JUDGE RANDALL
AND THE MURDER
TO BE SOLVED LATER

JUDGE RANDALL
AND THE MURDER
TO BE SOLVED LATER

TONY ROGERS

A Judge Randall Mystery

ISBN: 978-1-7356835-4-6 (Paperback)
ISBN: 978-1-7356835-5-3 (Ebook)

Published by Quinn Cove Books

Cover Design by Berge Design

To Tamara

1

Retired Judge Jim Randall hated reunions. He was proud of never having attended a single one – high school, college, or law school – until he was approaching seventy, and then only because Friday's reunion would pay homage to Stan Mitchell, a member of his law school class who had only a few months to live.

As a judge on the Massachusetts Superior Court, business had come to Jim; as an amateur detective, he had to stick his nose into other people's business. Considering that he was more of an introvert than an extrovert, such behavior didn't come naturally to him. He was happiest reading in his third floor study, drinking a contemplative coffee at The Long Gone, or having a quiet dinner with Pat Knowles – his former colleague on the bench and in retirement, his significant other. So why did he keep doing it? Ego? Pride? His contrarian streak? Or was it his lingering belief in justice, a belief that hadn't died even as he became more of a curmudgeon than ever? He didn't know the answer.

"What are you going to wear?" Pat asked in her Beacon Hill apartment on the night of the reunion (some nights they spent at Pat's, some nights at Jim's townhouse in Cambridge).

"I haven't seen some of these folks for years, I want to make a good impression. I'm thinking suit and tie."

"You'll be overdressed."

"Good. Let them be awed. Sure you don't want to come?"

"The only person who hates reunions more than you is me."

Jim walked the few blocks to the hotel where the reunion was being held. The streets of downtown Boston did not make any sense which made perfect sense to Jim; after a career's worth of logic, the lack thereof in Boston's streets was liberating.

The hotel was squeezed between classy old buildings and soulless new high-rises on a slight downslope not far from the Granary Burying Ground. The sound of traffic on nearby Tremont Street was loud, but on the side street Jim could hear his footsteps. He wished Pat were with him.

A mini-sonic boom of laughter and catch-up chatter knocked him back on his heels when he entered the crowded ballroom and for a moment he wanted to flee. But he straightened his tie and boldly stepped forward. Faces turned towards him...Jim? Jim Randall? Is that you? My god, Jim Randall! How are you? Where have you been?

"I'm not a fan of reunions."

"Then you've come to the right place," a former classmate whose name Jim had forgotten slapped him on the shoulder.

"I came because of Stan. What a shame."

"Real shame. Even assholes deserve better fates. Hey, you don't have a drink!"

"I just got here."

The man whose name would come back to Jim later pointed to the side of the room. "The bar is over there. Good luck fighting your way through the crowd."

Jim took his time wending his way to the bar. As long as he kept moving and looking over everyone's shoulder, he didn't have to make small talk. A few nods of recognition, a few startled glances. He reached the bar.

"Red wine, please."

While the young man poured, Jim surveyed the assemblage. What was wrong with him? His classmates were by and large nice people, so why was he being even more of a curmudgeon than usual? And what was the big deal with small talk anyway? He could fake it when he had to. He wished Pat were there, he felt safe when she was with him.

"Here you are, sir," the bartender was holding out a glass of red wine. Jim thanked him and took a sip. Domestic. Probably California, maybe Oregon. He much preferred wines from the Languedoc. This would have to do.

Out of the corner of his eye, he glimpsed the dais and saw a withered man in a wheelchair. The man looked like the ashes from a campfire. Stan Mitchell had been a feared litigator turned private equity boss who gave bankrupt companies a new coat of paint and a lube job and sold them to buyers who should have known better. It was hard to believe the ashes in the wheelchair had ever been feared, let alone loathed. Since receiving his death sentence, Stan had become philanthropic, donating millions to unsung charities. Gradually his reputation for loathsomeness changed and as he neared death, all was forgiven.

Jim approached. A petite dark-haired nurse stood at attention beside Stan's wheelchair. Jim waited until the man speaking to Stan departed.

"Hello, Stan, I'm Jim Randall. We were in a study group together in law school, second year."

Stan's eyes remained alive even if the rest of him looked dead. "And we were on a moot court team together, third year."

"Your memory is better than mine."

Stan smiled? Scowled? Hard to tell. His mouth moved as if wrapped in cellophane. "I'm the one who is dying, yet I remember better than you?"

"Guess so." Jim gripped what was left of Stan's bony shoulder. "Great to see you, Stan."

Stan wheezed when he spoke. "Bullshit, but no matter, too late now. I've got things wrong with me I didn't know existed. I'm a lexicon of diseases you don't want to get."

"Yet here you are, being honored. Big night."

"Still here. Enjoy me while you can." Stan cackled at his quip, even though it was as stale as he was.

There were others waiting to speak to Stan, so Jim stepped aside. But as he went, he heard Stan say in a near-whisper, "Don't believe your eyes."

Was that directed at him or the next well-wisher? Jim wasn't sure. He kept moving, blending into the crowd. Death pissed him off: so banal to the species, so devastating to the individual. What was it like? He would find out soon enough; sixty-nine wasn't young. He sighed and looked for someone to talk to. Did it take the specter of death to make Jim Randall outgoing?

Relief came in the form of a woman he had liked in law school, Jennifer Giles. From Queens, if Jim remembered correctly. She had been the girlfriend of one of his classmates, so she and Jim were never more than friends, but he remembered her fondly. He approached with a smile.

"Jennifer? Jim Randall, remember me?"

"For Christ's sake, Jim Randall! You look great."

"You lie, but thanks. You look great yourself."

"You never come to reunions. Why now?"

"A man can't change his mind?" said with a hint of guilt masquerading as spite.

"Did I touch a nerve? If I did, I'm truly sorry."

"Not a nerve, a truth, for which I feel guilty."

"I see your name in the papers now and again."

"Yes. If you have murders to solve, I'm your man."

At the sound of an amplified voice asking for everyone's attention, Jim turned towards the podium. A fleshy man with a broad smile was gripping the microphone in both hands. "Ladies, gentlemen, calm down. We have a classmate to honor tonight, and you know who he is, Stan Mitchell."

Cheers.

"Stan was known as a fierce competitor in law school. He beat most of us in moot court, was always prepared in class, was generally...," the MC turned towards Stan, "a pain in the ass."

Laughter. Stan cocked his head and seemed to smile, but the smile was so faint, it was hard to distinguish from a grimace.

"As all of you know, Stan's hit some bad luck lately and we're all here to honor him. I don't want to tire him out, so I'll keep this short. Stan, we love you, at least most of us do. I'm joking; we revere you, buddy. Let's raise our glasses and toast one of our own, Stan Mitchell."

Glasses raised high, heartfelt hip-hip-hoorays. Stan didn't stir. He sat slumped in his wheelchair, his head lolling to one side, eyes wide open, an expression of mild surprise on his lips. A murmur of concern rippled through the crowd.

"Stan? Stan?" The MC peered closer. "Oh my god! I need help up here."

A flurry of activity blocked Stan from Jim's sight. The crowd in the room seemed stunned. Absolute silence.

"Someone! Please! Call an ambulance!"

*

Pat was asleep when Jim got home. He hated to wake her.

"Pat? I'm sorry, but I've got to talk to you."

She stirred. "What is it?"

"Wake up please."

She struggled to sit up. "What is it? Are you okay?"

"No. Stan Mitchell died while he was being honored. He died while we watched. God, it was awful." Jim shuddered.

She was wide awake now. "Died? How?"

"Don't know. While we were toasting him. Gone. Just like that. Poof!"

"Let me wake up. That's horrible, Jim. Do they know the cause?"

"Heart attack or stroke, who knows? He had at least one prior heart attack that I know of, and I believe he suffered a major stroke years ago. But he had so many things wrong with him, it could be almost anything." Jim perched on the side of the bed. "Sorry to wake you. Go back to sleep."

"No, I'm awake now. I'll get up and make us some tea."

He gripped her hand. "He didn't make a sound. Didn't moan, didn't clutch his chest. Just lights out."

"Put your head on my shoulder," Pat said.

Jim's early life had not been easy. Emotionally distant father, mother who died way too early, a patchwork of unreliable relatives. He did not feel solid until he became a judge, and life events outside his courtroom could still rattle him inordinately. "I want to cry," he said on Pat's shoulder.

"Go ahead and cry."

"The great Jim Randall?" He lifted his head and studied her face. "I'm so lucky to have you."

"Yes, you are. Come to bed where you're safe."

2

Stan Mitchell's demise made the front of the Metro section of the Boston *Globe*. Noted in the story were Mitchell's financial success after leaving the law, his many philanthropies, his board memberships; soft-pedaled was his reputation for being despised by all he encountered.

The story was written by Sasha Cohen, who had helped Jim on several prior cases. She was a tenacious young reporter whom Jim met when she wrote for an alternative weekly which had since folded. Jim texted her after he read her story:

> *Stan Mitchell and I were law school classmates,*
> *and I was in the room when he died. Want to talk?*

Her reply came quickly:

> *Coffee at The Long Gone, 10 a.m. tomorrow?*

Since leaving the bench, The Long Gone had become Jim's de facto office. He did some of his best thinking in the badly lit Inman Square coffee shop. Harvard Square had long since become the home of women's clothing stores and banks, Kendall Square near MIT had become Silicon Valley East, but Inman Square, for now at least, remained proudly un-gentrified.

Sasha got to The Long Gone before Jim did. Since moving to the *Globe* she had become more cynical, but her fundamental nature remained positive. And she still loved being a journalist. "What's not to love about being paid to be nosy?" she had once said to him. She was sitting at a back table, near the restrooms.

"Hi, Jim."

"How are you, Sasha?"

The tired wooden chairs of The Long Gone creaked whenever they were pulled closer to a table. "Just great. Is it correct that Stan Mitchell died without sound or fury?"

"None that I could see or hear."

"Did people cheer?"

"Now, now, don't be cynical."

Sasha softened. "I've been up since 4 a.m., forgive me, but am I wrong to think he was hated?"

"No, you're not. In law school he was a pushy, insensitive asshole-in-training, and he perfected that persona during his career. What I never could figure out was whether he was obnoxious by nature or whether he adopted that persona to add fear to his arsenal. "

"Did you see anything unusual happen before he died?"

"Why? Do you think there is something suspicious about his death?"

"You were there, you tell me."

"I didn't think so at the time, and now that you put the idea in my head, I still don't. A nurse was keeping a close eye on him."

"Good. That settles it."

"Did somebody tell you otherwise?"

"There was speculation. A silent death as he's being honored?"

"It happens, Sasha."

"And so does murder."

"Yes, so does murder. But if I were pursuing this case, I'd rule out all possible natural causes before I leapt to murder."

"Will you pursue this case, Jim?"

"What case? First of all, I think this was death-as-usual. Secondly, I didn't like Stan and don't wish to spend time thinking about him. And thirdly, you cannot goad me into doing your leg work for you."

"But I've done yours for you in the past, haven't I?"

"Which I deserve, because I'm venerable."

Sasha laughed. "Were you an impartial judge or were you subject to flattery?"

Jim feigned a glare. "A fierce judge, and don't you forget it."

Jim walked home the long way, past Beauty Shop Row with its hair, nail, and skin salons – a dozen crammed into three blocks. The walk was twice as long as if he walked straight home, but touchstones mattered more to him as he aged. What delighted Jim about Beauty Shop Row was its sheer excess, its improbability.

He arrived home just as a #69 bus pulled to a stop on his corner. Uncanny timing, that bus. Sometimes he got the impression it was mocking him by being available only when he didn't need it.

Jim didn't say a word during dinner, which Pat knew was a sign he was mulling an idea that would sound nuts if uttered aloud. So she let him think in silence. After dinner, they read in his living room. Only when they were upstairs getting ready for bed did Jim speak his mind.

"Stan said something to me I'm trying to decipher. Don't believe your eyes, he said."

"What do you think he meant?"

"Probably nothing, but what if one of the many people who hated Stan Mitchell wanted to kill him and decided that the best place to do it was where murder would be least suspected? And what if Stan had a foreshadowing of his demise?"

"I wondered when you'd don your detective's hat. I could see the curiosity building in you."

"Nonsense. I didn't start to think about murder until Sasha Cohen put it in my mind."

"Politely and with deep affection, I say, bullshit. You were already thinking it when you got home last night after you witnessed Stan die."

"Oh, yeah?"

"Yeah."

"Okay, maybe you're right. But what do you think of my theory?"

"It sounds like a lawyerly way to murder. Has the medical examiner determined the cause of death?"

"Preliminary conclusion is arrhythmia. Mitchell had worn a pacemaker for years and it may have malfunctioned. Wouldn't that be perfect? Even Mitchell's pacemaker had it in for him. But I haven't ruled out murder. The possibility is too delicious."

"Oh, Jim, you are so transparent."

"What do you mean by that?"

"Go to sleep."

Pat turned out the light on her side of the bed.

He watched her turn on her side and close her eyes. "I can see you smiling," he said. "Don't."

"Goodnight, Jim."

"I mean it, don't."

"I'm not."

"You'd better not be."

"Now I'm smiling. Goodnight, Jim."

*

In the morning he called the head of the Boston office of the FBI. Enrique Montgomery was considerably younger than he, casual in dress, professional in manner. Paid due deference to Jim's judicial experience but didn't cater to him.

"Haven't heard from you in a while," Enrique said over the phone.

"And I probably shouldn't be bothering you now."

"What's up?"

"I assume you heard about the man who died at his law school reunion? I was there. He was my classmate."

"I read about it. Why?"

"The villain was his pacemaker, according to the medical examiner. Does that sit well with you?"

"Jim, I haven't thought about it."

"Think about it now, for old times' sake." Enrique and Jim had collaborated on cases before.

"Okay, I'm thinking about it, and I still see nothing suspicious."

"Me neither, which is what makes me suspicious. The timing seems too coincidental to be coincidental."

"Why? The law of averages says that a pacemaker will fail during a law school reunion once in a while."

"When the man with the pacemaker being honored on stage is hated by his classmates?"

"How does one tamper with a pacemaker?" Enrique thought for a second, then answered his own question. "I guess it's possible if the battery pack is worn externally."

"Do we know if that was true of Stan Mitchell's?"

"Jim, until you called a moment ago I knew nothing about Stan Mitchell, let alone whether his battery pack was external or internal. My understanding – admittedly sketchy – is that external packs are only used when the recipient is too weak to withstand the surgical procedure to implant the pacemaker internally. If Mitchell had a pacemaker for years that would be unlikely, but even if he wore an external battery pack, how could anyone tamper with it without Mitchell's knowledge? I have to say – as much as I respect you – that murder by pacemaker seems farfetched to me. Sorry."

"Maybe I need to take a break from sleuthing, is that what you're saying?"

"I wouldn't dare. You are hardwired to meddle."

Jim took his meddling self to The Long Gone, where he sat wondering what had happened to his appreciation of chance. Coincidences didn't necessarily have to arouse suspicion. Get a grip, Jim.

Jim went to the counter to order a refill, and while waiting texted Ernie Farrell, his computer guru.

> *Can pacemakers be hacked by a computer whiz like you?*

Ernie's answer arrived after Jim carried his refill back to the table:

> *I doubt it. Why? Looking to knock somebody off?*

That night, Jim and Pat ate at a trendy new restaurant (itself a trend) in Inman Square. The restaurant offered small plates (tidbits being de rigueur among foodies) but also featured some dinner-size dishes. Jim was equally appalled by overflowing plates at the chain restaurants and tiny nibbles at the trendy places. What was wrong with a pork chop? And did green always have to mean kale? Jim and Pat were enjoying their dinners when Ernie replied:

> *Most pacemaker failures stem from dead batteries or dislodged electrodes. Hacking is next to impossible.*

"I give up," Jim remarked after he read Ernie's text. "Looks like I have to accept that Stan Mitchell died a natural death, as delightful as the thought of his murder is."

"Poor Jim."

"On second thought...." Jim pulled out his phone and texted Jennifer Giles.

"What are you doing?" Pat asked.

"Texting a classmate I spoke to at the reunion. Her ex-husband was a friend of Stan's in law school."

Jennifer texted back as they were waiting for their check.

Jim looked up from reading her message. "She'll meet me tomorrow at The Long Gone."

"What do you hope to discover?"

"The unexpected."

*

Jennifer Giles looked out of place in The Long Gone. Her pantsuit was far smarter than what most women wore in the coffee shop and her face showed a hint of makeup. "I'm not over the shock of seeing Stan die. Are you?" she asked.

"No, I'm not. My mother died after a short illness when I was 13. My father died suddenly while I was in college. Death for me was something that happened in a hospital or an ambulance, not on a dais, in front of an audience."

She cocked her head. "How are you, Jim? You were such an earnest young man in law school."

"Earnest? How about lost?"

"All but a few of us were. But you didn't try to hide it, like most of us did. I admired that."

"I didn't have the acting skills. How are you doing?"

Jennifer smiled. "I'm doing well. My second husband and I have been married for 29 years, can you believe that?"

"That's wonderful, Jennifer. What I wanted to talk to you about was your first husband and his friendship with Stan Mitchell. They knew each other well in law school, didn't they?"

"Jack? Yes, Jack and Stan joined the Federalist Society together. They shared a belief that government should get out of their way so they could become powerful and rich."

"Which Stan succeeded in doing and Jack didn't, if I remember correctly?"

"Yes, Jack became a gadfly to those in power but remained an irritant rather than a player. He became more and more bitter until he was impossible to live with. I divorced him after seven years."

"What did you see in Jack to begin with?"

"Ambition, self-confidence. I lacked both. And he had charisma then."

"After you divorced, did you have any contact with him?"

"Very little."

"Enough to know if he stayed friends with Stan Mitchell?"

"Not really."

"Not really you didn't have enough contact with him to know, or not really he didn't stay friends with Stan?"

"Let me think." Jennifer turned her gaze to the front of The Long Gone, where a window above a three-stool counter overlooked busy Cambridge Street. "I remember running into Jack at a fundraiser about a year ago. No, two years. We did the catching up with old friends routine and Jack mentioned seeing Stan recently and noting how sick he was."

"Did Jack mention whether Stan seemed despondent?"

"What are you getting at?"

"I'm wondering if Stan's death was due to pacemaker failure as the coroner said. I'm wondering if Stan – knowing he didn't have long to live – decided to end his life at a time and place of his choosing instead of letting death call the shots, and being a showman, chose to do so in front of an audience."

Jennifer peered closely at Jim. "Your reputation on the bench and in law school was for being no nonsense. Apparently one can fall off the bench as hard as one can fall off the wagon."

Jim smiled. "Deep end, huh?"

Jennifer pursed her lips. "Speaking of which, The Long Gone doesn't strike me as you, at least not the you I knew in law school. You were serious to a fault, sullen even. I can't imagine you wasting time in a coffee house."

"Are you the same as you were in law school?"

"Better." She smiled. "Gotta go. If I remember anything else I'll let you know."

Jim called Pat from the sidewalk outside The Long Gone. As he waited for her to answer, a fire truck pulled out of the corner fire station. "What are you doing right now?" he asked Pat.

"What?" she said. "I can't hear you over the siren."

The siren took itself down Cambridge Street towards Harvard. "I asked, what are you doing right now?"

"Jotting notes for another book."

"Really?"

"Why do you sound shocked?"

"Because you haven't mentioned a second book."

"Yes, I have. You just haven't listened."

"What's this one about?"

"It's about nothing so far. I just started."

"Do you want me to help?"

"Like you did on *Bench Life*, which we were supposed to write together?"

"Yeah, like that, which turned out to be a breeze."

"Because you didn't do anything."

"I guess that could explain it. Your place tonight?"

"Sounds good."

"Can I come over now?"

"I detect lust in your voice."

"Lust? How about the floundering of a tired old man seeking purpose in life."

"Sounds like lust to me."

When Jim walked to Pat's from The Long Gone, he liked to cut over to Broadway and cross the Charles River on the Longfellow Bridge, rather than on the truncated bridge by the Science Museum. The view from the Longfellow Bridge was expansive rather than cramped, and to get there he had to navigate the tightknit streets behind the courthouse, which pleased him. He had walked every one of those tangled streets during his time on the bench and loved them.

He couldn't rid his mind of the idea of Mitchell committing suicide in front of an unsuspecting audience. What a way to go. Having received a sentence of death by illness, which must have infuriated control-freak Stan, he chose to control the narrative of his demise and chose a time and place that would make his death the stuff of legend.

But, Jim, my man, if true, wouldn't Stan leave a note, a tweet, some explanation, however cryptic, of his actions? Choose a form of explanation that would tantalize and mystify the largest possible audience for the longest stretch of time? Jim didn't notice the broad Charles when he crossed, so absorbed was he in speculation, and as he climbed Beacon Hill to Pat's he must have been grinning because Pat greeted him at the door with, "What's so funny?"

He stepped inside her spotless apartment. "Funny?"

"You're grinning. You don't grin. Why are you grinning?"

"What if Stan Mitchell committed suicide?"

"That makes you grin?"

"What if he fooled everybody?"

"Why would be do that?"

"To have the last laugh one last time."

"Why would he care?"

"The ultimate victory for an ultra-competitive man."

"That theory would be thrown out of court."

"Only by stiff-necked judges like you."

They sat down on her sofa. He waited a beat, then put his arm around her.

"What has gotten into you?" she said.

"You said it on the phone."

"Lust?"

"Yes, ma'am. And don't you dare gavel it out of order."

3

The morning sun fell across the *Boston Globe*, the glare making the headlines hard to read. The *Globe* seemed to shrink daily, but Jim still loved it. He liked local news, especially political and legal news, and to an extent, sports. He wasn't a devout sports fan, which made him an anomaly in the Boston area, but he did like the Red Sox. He liked them best when they were perennial underdogs, but he liked them okay when they won.

He moved the paper on the table so it was out of the sun and turned to the business section, where he learned that Arthur Maplewood, a pioneer in the now-thriving organic foods business, had died of complications of diabetes at the age of 71.

"Didn't Arthur Maplewood pass through your court at some point?" he said without looking up from the paper.

"What are you looking at?" Pat answered.

He slid the paper so she could see. "Arthur Maplewood died. Wasn't yours the court of first instance in a lawsuit involving him years ago?"

She looked up from the paper. "Yes, a private equity firm was attempting a hostile takeover of his company, Maplewood Naturals, and Arthur Maplewood fought back hard."

"I remember you telling me about the suit during one of our lunches in the cafeteria, when we were chaste and sedate."

"Ahh, the courthouse cafeteria! The good old days."

Pat rarely used exclamation points when she spoke. Her mind was lively, but her manner restrained. Jim took note of what prompted the use of an exclamation point now: the courthouse cafeteria.

Jim poured himself more coffee. Talking as he poured, he said, "Just out of curiosity, who ran the private equity firm that tried to acquire Maplewood Naturals?"

"Stan Mitchell."

"That's what I thought. Mitchell died less than a week ago. Think there's a connection with Maplewood's death?"

"I know how your mind works. You love symmetry. When you see a possible connection between seemingly unrelated events, you become as excited as a little boy. Here you've got two fierce business rivals dying within days of each other, one of whom died while being honored by his classmates, and mental sparks fly."

"Think you know me, do you?" Jim brought his coffee back to the table – the sun had risen far enough so it no longer cast a glare on the *Globe*. "Okay, so I like connections. Is that so wrong? What if there is one here? Wouldn't that be wonderful?"

*

The memorial service for Stan Mitchell was held within walking distance of Jim's house, which improved Mitchell's standing in Jim's mind. The church was crowded with mourners, sincere and otherwise. Mitchell had been cremated, so the question of open or closed casket didn't present itself. If Mitchell had relatives there, they stayed hidden. The memorial service had been arranged by Mitchell's business partners.

The service was brief. The minister said the usual things, a law partner praised Stan's rapier legal mind, a beneficiary of Stan's late-life philanthropy praised his generosity, and Stan's younger brother cited his work ethic. Nobody praised his kindness.

Jim made a point of walking home via Harvard Square, so called even though it resembled two sides of an isosceles triangle rather than a square. The Square's funky days were long gone: today's Harvard Square had more banks than diners or bars, but it remained lively, and death being Jim's leitmotif for the day, he wanted an infusion of life. Out of Town News by the subway entrance was one of the few remaining vestiges of Old Harvard Square but there were rumors it was not long for this world; money, you know. Death and profit, the eternal verities. He stopped in front of one wall of new magazines and looked for something silly to read. The love child of a current bachelorette was the cover story on many of the magazines.

Whose Baby Is Lisa Carrying?
Rick wants to know before he pops the question

Which was carrying silly too far even for Jim's present mood. He scanned the covers of the business journals, searching for a mention of the Mitchell-Maplewood deaths. Nope. Nothing. Neither silly nor serious for Jim today.

To support his local newsstand, he bought an armload of magazines he didn't need, and took them home. Once there, he dumped them in his recycling bin and called Jennifer Giles. They agreed to meet for lunch the next day.

The restaurant where they met had window walls that overlooked historic Brattle Street, but what Jim and

Jennifer Giles saw from their table was a narrow dry cleaner, a narrow barber shop, and a sliver of a pizza place.

Jennifer Giles seemed less business-like the second time around. Calmer in gaze, as if she had more time, and friendlier, as if she had decided Jim was trustworthy.

"After we talked I wondered if I know more about Stan Mitchell than I initially remembered," she began.

"And?"

"I remembered his contempt for people other than himself. I remember he and Jack used to argue endlessly about matters they basically agreed on. They loved to butt heads, subject matter not important. At the time I was impressed by their mental toughness, but in retrospect they seem like little boys trying to be men. Aren't men who pick fights little boys by definition? I can't see Stan expiring without butting a head or two."

Outside the window, a flash of red scarf on a passing pedestrian interrupted a steady stream of Cambridge drab. Jim mused, "Maybe Stan decided to butt heads with death. He knew his health was terrible. It's possible he miscalculated, but I think he intended to die in a way guaranteed to add to the Legend of Stan Mitchell. Death is ho-hum, Stan Mitchell is one-of-a-kind. The other possibility is that he was done in by somebody with a grudge or a score to settle."

Jennifer twirled the stem of her wine glass. "You are really working this, aren't you?"

"Curiosity is my fatal flaw. In law school, did Stan's Federalist views ever veer into weirdness? Outlandish conspiracy theories, perhaps?"

"Oh, sure," Jennifer said. "Listening to Stan and Jack uncage their demons was to be entertained and weirded out simultaneously. It seemed like a game at the time. They would get more and more wound up, and I'd start to be appalled, then they'd laugh out loud and high five each other. Boys will be boys."

"But they grow up to be men, men with unrestrained egos and childlike appetites. Men like that are dangerous."

"Men like Stan Mitchell and my ex. I take your point."

*

Jim relied on two mental touchstones to keep him grounded. One was Cicero, whom he didn't always agree with but whose clear thinking he admired. The other was Pat, whom he also didn't always agree with but whose opinion he always took seriously. In lieu of Cicero, he ran his thoughts by Pat that night.

"I believe Jennifer Giles is honest," he said to Pat in bed before they turned out the lights. "But she holds a grudge against her ex, and I think that affects her judgement...."

"Are you okay?"

"Yes, why?"

"Because you stopped in the middle of a thought."

"I was just thinking, why am I getting involved? No one except me thinks the two deaths were anything but coincidental. And no one, not a soul, suspects as I do, that at least one of the deaths was murder. So what the hell am I doing? Why am I wasting my time?"

He gave Pat a little smile, which was a change from when he was on the bench and perpetually serious.

"I mean it," he emphasized. "What do I think I'm doing?"

"I'm stunned. Losing heart? What has happened to you?"

"I have seen the light." Jim got out of bed. "I'm going to read in my study."

"You can read here. I'll turn on the light."

"No, you go to sleep."

He climbed the stairs to the third floor. His study, which looked out the rear of the house, was the sole finished room on the third floor. Other than the study, there was a storage closet where he stored personal records he no longer needed but couldn't bear to part with, and a clothes closet where his judicial robes hung in effigy. His aerie, his sanctuary.

He settled into his leather chair and picked a book from the table beside the chair. His eyes went out the window to the night sky, never completely dark in the city. He felt good with his decision. No backsliding, he told himself; Stan Mitchell's death does not concern you. Stay out of it.

He fell asleep in his chair without reading a word.

Sometime in the middle of the night, Pat came upstairs and woke him.

"Jim?" She squeezed his shoulder. "Jim, you fell asleep. Come downstairs to bed."

Jim roused himself. "What time is it?"

"Almost 3."

He gingerly pushed himself upright.

"Are you okay?" Pat asked. "Do you feel okay?"

"I feel fine."

Jim followed Pat downstairs. As he climbed into bed, he said, "I'll say this out loud so you can hold me to it. I am not going to tilt at Stan Mitchell's windmill any longer."

*

Vermont beckoned. Pat didn't want to come. "The words for my next book are starting to flow and I don't want to interrupt them. Do you mind?"

"Far be it for me to interrupt flow. Anyway, a little time alone will help me firm up my resolve to stay out of this case."

Their Vermont house (his house, technically, but he now thought of it as theirs) was close to the top of the ridge but shielded from western winds. He treasured the view of the Connecticut River valley from the living/dining room.

He dropped his bag inside the door and turned on the lights. A small part of him was always surprised to find the house as he left it.

He sat down in the living room looking out the expansive windows and called Pat. "I made it," he said. "The house is the same. How are you? Words flowing?"

"No, they are drip, drip, dripping."

"Probably because I'm not there."

"Undoubtedly."

"I miss you."

A minor chuckle. "*You* were the one who wanted to get away. To 'firm up your resolve,' you said."

"You didn't have to let me go."

"I think that quip has broken the logjam. I can feel the words starting to flow."

"Then I'll get out of their way. Talk to you later."

He remained in his chair after he got off the line. The drive wasn't long but he wasn't getting any younger, and it tired him more lately. Sitting felt good.

His phone did its thing. He couldn't stand his ringtone but was too lazy to change it. He assumed Pat had forgotten something she wanted to say.

"Hi, couldn't stand not hearing my voice, huh?"

The voice on the other end of the line sounded bewildered. "Jim? Is that you?"

"Who is this?"

"Sasha Cohen. Everything all right?"

"I'm embarrassed. I thought you were Pat. We had just been talking to each other."

"No, it's me, and I have some news about Stan Mitchell's death."

"Sasha, I'm not interested any longer. I've decided it's a dead end, and besides, it's none of my business."

"I must admit I'm surprised. Your doggedness usually has you on a short leash. Do you want to hear my news anyway?"

"Sure, no harm in that."

"I have a source in the medical examiner's office, who confirmed that arrhythmia was the cause of death. The new thing I learned is that apparently Mitchell had stopped taking his blood pressure medication. There was no indication of it in his system, which means he had stopped taking it days, if not weeks, before his death."

"Could that have been the cause of death?"

"According to my source, no, but it could've contributed to his death. But why would he have stopped taking it?

Did he know he was going to die, so why bother taking his meds?"

"Thank you for letting me know, but I meant what I said, I'm done with Stan Mitchell."

"Suit yourself." She stopped short. "Really? You don't think this lends weight to the possibility he killed himself?"

"Maybe, but it's also possible that he simply forgot to take his medication. He lived alone, remember? No one to remind him to take his pills."

"I hear a spark of interest."

"A spark but no flame. Good luck, Sasha. When I get back to Cambridge, let's have lunch."

He stood at the window when he got off the phone. The afternoon clouds looked in no hurry to move. The river shimmered.

He turned and carried his bag into the bedroom, trying to rid his mind of Sasha's tantalizing phone call.

He took himself to his favorite inn for dinner. No one wore ties in Vermont, but he donned the worn blazer he kept in Vermont. A judge's robe, a worn blazer; he felt more comfortable with a covering.

He lingered over his first glass of Côtes du Rhône for a long time before ordering, letting his legal mind dwell on the menu. What menus needed for non-foodies like him were footnoted citations in simple language – How does this dish taste? Can it be compared to other foods? Will I like it?

He ordered chicken – simple roast chicken – and another glass of wine. Without a murder to be solved, he quickly got bored and wondered why on earth he hadn't brought something to read as he usually did when he ate alone. Yes, he could read his phone, but he hated, *hated*, to read from a small screen. It felt like punishment, like being forced to read through a keyhole.

He skipped desert and coffee and drove home in a funk. The twisting road played havoc with his sense of direction. Darkness squeezed his car; no moon, not even a star. Fortunately he knew the way even in the dark and got home safely. He collapsed on the sofa and called Pat.

"I ate at the inn. What about you?"

"At home. In my kitchen. You sound out of breath."

"Harrowing journey. The dark, you know."

"Ah, yes, the dark. There should be a law."

Life returned to him. "Don't make fun of me. I need something to do, something to occupy my time, now that I'm out of the Stan Mitchell business. Help me."

"Would you like me to compile a list of your obsessions for you to choose from?"

"That would be helpful, thank you."

"How long do you think you'll stay up there?"

"Once here, I acclimate fast. I'll probably stay three or four days."

"Let me know."

As it turned out, he returned in two. He missed Pat.

"I missed you," he told her at her apartment.

"I don't believe you."

He hugged her. "No, I did, Pat."

She leaned back to look at him. "What brought this on?"

He smiled the devious smile of a judge with a gavel and the last word. "Are you objecting?"

"Not at all."

"Because if you are, I will hold you in contempt. I'm tired."

"Are you coming down with something?"

"No, the drive from Vermont tires me out more than it used to."

He went into the kitchen and returned with a glass of ice water. "I think I'll sit for a while." He chose the sofa. He sat for a minute, then reached in his pocket for his phone.

"Who are you calling?"

"Sasha Cohen."

"You said you wouldn't."

"I said I wouldn't get caught up in a wild goose chase. I didn't say I wouldn't check on how the goose chase is going."

Sasha was on the other line but said she'd call Jim back. When she did she asked if Jim had new information.

"No, I'm not pursuing it any longer, remember?"

"The question is, do you remember?"

"You and Pat. Yes, I do."

"Well, in case you're interested, I dug deeper in Stan Mitchell's business record and discovered a complaint had been filed against him with the attorney general six months ago. It's still pending. Guess who the complainant is?"

"Arthur Maplewood."

"How did you guess?"

"I'm good at making connections. I should have been a couples counselor."

"You'd be great. So, are you back to pursuing the truth about Mitchell and Maplewood?"

"No, I'll leave it to you and your esteemed newspaper to pursue whether the deaths of the two men have any connection, while I stretch out on Pat's sofa and enjoy my retirement."

*

Jim was overdue for lunch with his friend, Ted Conover, and arranged to meet him the following week. Ted's office was near the courthouse – draw a straight line from Jim's house to The Long Gone and on to the courthouse, and Ted's office would lie to the left of the line on the Somerville border. Territory as familiar to Jim as the interior of his former courtroom.

They had known each other since Ted was a brand new Assistant District Attorney and Jim a recently appointed judge. Ted was only a few years younger than Jim, but looked a dozen years younger.

"Someday you're going to look your age," Jim said.

Ted had no discernable sense of humor but could respond to a jibe like the good lawyer he was: "I donated my wrinkles to you to give you gravitas."

The deli where they ate was mostly takeout, but there were a few vinyl top tables. Jim and Ted sat at the only empty table.

"What unsolved case is obsessing you currently, Jim?"

"I'm on hiatus, but I confess I'm interested in the near-simultaneous deaths of Stan Mitchell and Arthur Maplewood."

"Me too."

"My friend Sasha Cohen tells me that Arthur Maplewood had lodged an ethics complaint against Mitchell six months ago."

"Does she allege a connection between the deaths?"

"She wonders, as do I. But I'm tired of chasing wild geese."

"And I don't have the manpower. Plus, it's too speculative even if I did. I need something concrete. This case seems tailor-made for a freelance snoop like you."

"Trouble is, Ted, when a freelance snoop like me gets involved in a case, he annoys by-the-book guys like you, and when the freelance snoop refuses to get involved, he annoys by-the-book guys who want the help of someone who thinks outside the box."

"What can I tell you? You're annoying," Ted said with a by-the-book look on his face.

"Have you uncovered anything suspicious about Arthur Maplewood's death?"

"I thought you'd never ask."

"Have you?"

"No. But if I were a freelance snoop, that's where I'd dig next."

*

"Ted seemed intrigued by the idea of a connection between the deaths of Mitchell and Maplewood," Jim reported to Pat that evening.

They were reading in Jim's livingroom after dinner. "So now you're back on the case?"

"I only spoke to Ted as a favor to Sasha. I'm not back in."

"Right." She hid her smile in her book.

After a minute in which her head remained in her book, Jim grew exasperated. "Okay, I'm tempted, I admit. Are you happy?"

She looked up with a straight face. A less dignified woman would have batted her eyes. "What?"

He shook his head. "Never mind."

She sighed. Dramatically. "Get involved or not, as you please."

"Now it's a matter of pride not to, even if I wanted to."

"Any reason other than pride?"

"Flimsy-to-nonexistent evidence."

"That hasn't stopped you before when you get a whiff of malfeasance."

"That's just the point. No whiff this time, only the silent churning of windmills, which I'm tired of chasing."

"Then you've made a wise decision." She lowered her head into her book again.

He waited. Nothing. "What are you reading?"

"Jane Gardam. A British novelist with a light touch and a wicked tongue."

"I don't know her work."

"My favorite of hers is *Old Filth*, about an 80-year-old judge who turns crotchety in retirement."

Jim rarely failed to respond to Pat's jibes, so when he didn't respond she inquired, "Jim? Everything okay?"

"Ted filled me in on the feud between Stan Mitchell and Arthur Maplewood. It began when Mitchell attempted to acquire Maplewood Naturals, which was – for Mitchell – an unnatural act. He usually went after failing companies, and Maplewood Naturals was thriving. Arthur Maplewood successfully fought off Mitchell's attempt, then six months ago, filed an ethics complaint against Mitchell for his tactics in the takeover attempt, which must have absolutely infuriated Mitchell."

"I knew it."

"Knew what?"

"Your next step will be to convene your brain trust of Sasha Cohen and Ernie Farrell while still denying being involved."

"Sounds like a plan," Jim said, reaching for his phone.

4

Jim, Sasha, and Ernie Farrell met at The Long Gone midmorning two days later. Midmorning at The Long Gone was the hour for earbuds and laptops – coffee shop as Amtrak quiet car. The three stealth-inquisitors commandeered a table near the restrooms, away from the pitter-patter of thumbs and keyboards.

Speaking quietly, Jim explained the reason for the meeting, "The near-simultaneous deaths of Stan Mitchell and Arthur Maplewood caught my attention, but what sustains my interest is the personal and professional animosity between the two men: Mitchell's hostile takeover attempt of Maplewood's company, and the ethics complaint Maplewood subsequently filed against Mitchell. Maybe both were business as usual, but increasingly it looks personal to me. The only thing that's missing is evidence of murder, but you can't have everything."

Straight-arrow Ernie looked puzzled, sardonic-Sasha smiled.

"What do you want from us?" Ernie asked.

"Yes," Sasha echoed. "What are you asking us to do?"

"Over the course of his career, Stan Mitchell went from being a jerk in law school to a cutthroat litigator who took no prisoners to the head of a private equity firm that acquired bankrupt companies then resold them after laying off large numbers of staff, all but destroying the original company. In most cases, the shrunken companies folded after several years of struggle, but by then, Mitchell had made his bundle. This technique often led to bitter feelings, to say the least, but he seemed to relish them – better to be hated than ignored. Then, before he died, Mitchell's firm was trying to acquire Arthur Maplewood's company, a thriving company, unlike his usual prey. The ethics complaint was still pending at the time of Mitchell's and Maplewood's deaths. What I'm wondering is why Mitchell deviated from his usual practice of acquiring low-hanging fruit? Why did he go after Maplewood's company? For purely business reasons? Because he had a personal grudge against Maplewood? Maybe the attempted acquisition was revenge for something Maplewood had done to Mitchell."

"Revenge sounds right," Ernie said. "Didn't Mitchell have three wives? Are we sure Maplewood didn't have something to do with one or more of Mitchell's failed marriages?"

"Okay, anything personal or professional that caused the two men to hate each other. Jealousy, avarice, pride. Juicy stuff."

Sasha did a double take. "Judge Randall, the eminent jurist asking us to find juicy stuff? Fess up, what have you done with our beloved Jim?"

Jim looked pleased with himself. "Jim Randall, unleashed."

Ernie said, earnestly, "I'll check out the ethics complaint."

Jim shook his head. "I already tried. The complaint has been sealed."

Sasha: "I'll check our newspaper's morgue and see what I can find on the struggle between the two men."

"Good. Thanks. We shall now join hands and sing the amateur sleuths anthem."

Sasha slid back her chair. "Goodbye, Jim."

Ernie quickly followed.

Jim sang softly. "Oh, follow the leads, ye sleuths proud and tall, follow them, follow them, follow them all!" Jim chuckled at himself.

Ernie and Sasha had gone so didn't hear him but several coffee drinkers did and weren't pleased. Frowns, scowls and dirty looks from the patrons of The Long Gone.

*

The public record was easy to find even for a technophobe like Jim. A quick Google search revealed that Arthur Maplewood had been one of the first to recognize the profit potential in organic foods, and by starting Maplewood Naturals to distribute the produce of small growers in New England he had changed the business model from farm stands to supermarkets. The company did so well that over the next decade it acquired two dozen related companies and became a regional powerhouse in the food business. Eventually the company went public and its stock held its own or rose in value until Stan Mitchell's hostile takeover attempt, which spooked investors. Why was Mitchell, the bankruptcy king, trying to acquire a profitable company like Maplewood Naturals? Wall Street wanted to know, suspected skullduggery, grew wary. The simultaneous deaths of Mitchell and Maplewood sealed the company's fate, and its stock dropped in value. What Jim couldn't find in the public record was evidence of a personal feud between Mitchell and Maplewood. If animosity existed between them, it had been kept out of the public eye.

Sasha and Ernie had no trouble digging up dirt, reporting to Jim that the hostility between the two men had become so virulent that each refused to appear at any charity event the other was to attend. On one occasion – a fund-raiser for special needs kids – the organizers slipped up and invited the two men, who showed up simultaneously and nearly came to blows.

"I'm amazed that stayed out of the press," Jim said to Pat at her apartment. "Someone had good press aides."

"Both men were philanthropic. I'm sure that weighed in their favor."

"I wonder if anyone on Maplewood's management team will talk to me?"

"Tread lightly, Jim. His death was very recent. Feelings will still be raw."

*

Maplewood Naturals was headquartered in a former factory building just off I-93, a short hop to the airport and points north. The man who had agreed to meet with Jim was Maplewood Naturals chief operating officer. His name was John Gibbons.

"You said over the phone that you are a retired judge who, for your own reasons, is looking into the deaths of my late boss and Stan Mitchell."

The way Gibbons said it made clear he wanted to know more about Jim's purpose. How to explain? "I have unofficially helped solve several crimes since my retirement.

I didn't seek out that role but found I enjoy it, so I help the DA and FBI whenever I can."

Gibbons replied cautiously. "All right, but why these two deaths?"

"I was in the room when Stan Mitchell died. It was so unexpected, so wordless, I wanted to know more. The official explanation didn't persuade."

"But why Arthur's death? What's the connection?"

"There may be none, but Mitchell's attempted takeover of Maplewood Naturals and both men dying in the same week gives me pause."

Gibbons folded his hands beneath his chin. After a moment, he unfolded his hands. "What do you want to know?"

"What kind of a man was Arthur Maplewood? What was he like to work for?"

Gibbons shifted his weight in his chair. "A good man. Easy to work with. Fair minded, mild mannered, except when something he believed in was threatened and then... watch out!"

"Watch out, how? What would he do?"

"Go ballistic. Maplewood Naturals went public a dozen years ago. The Class A stock went to Arthur, giving him 10 votes for every share of stock he owned, which meant he retained control of the company. Stan Mitchell's private equity group started a stealth campaign to buy shares of ordinary stock from individual investors and pension funds. When Arthur became aware of the campaign, Mitchell had almost succeeded in buying enough shares to oust Arthur from control of his company."

"That must have infuriated him."

"To put it mildly."

"Did he express an opinion of Stan Mitchell personally?"

"Yes, a gusher of unprintable words that children are taught never to say, muttered at lightning speed, with barely a pause for breath. An impressive display of anger from a mild-mannered man. He was still fuming the day of his death."

"Did you see him that day? How did he seem physically?"

"Yes, he came into the office as usual. Other than a red face and bulging veins when I updated him on the takeover attempt, nothing seemed out of the ordinary. Arthur was a large man but not robust. He got sick often, was out for days. I teased him about running a natural foods company and having a weak constitution."

"Did he harbor bad feelings about others besides Mitchell? Was he a man of grudges?"

"No to both questions. That was what was so striking about his feud with Stan Mitchell. Arthur couldn't seem to let it go."

They talked for another fifteen minutes. As they shook hands, Gibbons asked, "Has this been helpful?"

"Yes. I don't yet know how, but yes."

Jim walked out of the building into a clear, brisk morning. The ground rumbled from the constant I-93 traffic. He stood where he was for a minute before heading to his car and home.

In his study that afternoon, he Googled Arthur Maplewood again. He already knew the basics – a widower at the time of his death, one son, one daughter, no other living relatives, one hundred percent devoted to work to the exclusion of vacations and hobbies. What Jim hoped to find was a quirk, an unlikely cause, a bizarre belief – something that could provide a spark of insight into a hidden side of Maplewood – but he couldn't find one. He consoled himself by saying that if a computer maestro like Ernie Farrell hadn't found such a quirk, it was unlikely that he, Jim Randall, whose computer skills began and ended with Google, would be able to.

Jim spent the night at Pat's, and in the morning he walked down the backside of Beacon Hill to Government Center and the FBI office. Enrique Montgomery was out of town, but Jim was a known commodity in his office and the receptionist, Fran, was one of the nicest people in the universe.

"Is there anyone besides Mr. Montgomery who can help you, Judge?"

"Yes. Somebody from forensics."

"We mainly rely on DC for our forensics, but let me check."

Jim was put in touch with a man in the local office who had the permanently furrowed brow and downcast eyes of someone for whom life is a perennial disappointment. "Fran said I should help you any way I can. What can I do for you?"

"If I wanted to kill somebody without leaving a trace, how would I do it?"

The man's expression didn't budge. "Do you have a particular person in mind?"

Jim smiled for him. "I watched a man die in front a ballroom of people. The official ruling was that death resulted from a faulty pacemaker. That doesn't ring true, and I'm searching for alternate explanations."

"There are several kinds of poison that are hard to detect if one doesn't know what to look for and where in the body to look. Arsenic was Agatha Christie's favorite."

"The man I watched die gave no signs of distress. A silent death. His head lolled to one side and he expired."

"Are you sure it was murder?"

"Not at all. It may have been suicide, he may have died from natural causes. He was a sick man. Many things could have killed him. The only thing I'm sure of is he died."

"If the medical examiner had no reason to think a crime was committed, he or she might not have looked for hard-to-trace poisons. So your theory could be correct, but without knowing more, I'm not sure how else I can help you."

"I'm grateful to you for indulging me. Here's my card. If you think of anything else, I'd appreciate a call."

Jim walked up the backside of Beacon Hill, eyes on his feet, mind on murder. Arthur Maplewood seemed an unlikely killer, but then again, mild-mannered men who are provoked beyond what they can tolerate are capable of explosive acts of violence. He had seen examples of that in court. The possibility of losing Maplewood Naturals to a jerk like Stan Mitchell must have been the worst form of provocation.

Jim reached the top of the hill. The gold dome of the statehouse loomed above his left shoulder. Downhill to the right for a short block and he reached Pat's.

Jim was turning his key in the front door lock when his phone rang. He paused on the stoop and looked at his phone. He didn't recognize the number – probably an annoyance call. He felt like yelling at someone, so he answered.

"Judge Randall?" A male voice.

"Who is this?"

"Doesn't matter. I have information about Stan Mitchell that might interest you."

Jim hesitated. He was leery of anonymous tips but something about this man's voice intrigued him. "Who are you and how did you get my number?"

"Who I am is unimportant. How did I get your number? From one of the people you have helped since leaving the bench."

"Go ahead, I'm listening."

5

Jim never learned the man's name. He said he had worked for Stan Mitchell years ago, reunited with him six years before Stan's death, then fell out again. Now he wanted to set the record straight.

As Jim sat down in Pat's living room he said to the caller, "Go ahead. I'm listening."

The man on the phone said, "I was one of the bright young business school grads Stan hired to assist him when his private equity venture gained traction. We were assigned potential acquisitions to assess and were told to always ask ourselves how quickly a company could be flipped and resold. I enjoyed the work. Stan was a demanding boss and could be a mean son of a bitch, but he wasn't mean to be mean. It was a question of being focused on the goal of making money and growing Stan's ego. Anyone that got in Stan's way became his enemy. And that included at least one of his wives. Maybe all three, I don't know. But I did know his second wife, Isabel, who he married a month after his first marriage broke up. When Isabel talks to me about Stan, she heaps scorn on him."

The caller paused.

"Go on," Jim said. "You've got my attention."

"Stan treated women as a means to an end. His first and third wives were stunning and looked great on his arm at galas. He was very proud of them. Isabel was different. When I went to work for him, he and Isabel were just starting to get serious about each other. He said very little about her, which I was later told was highly unusual. He bragged incessantly about his first and third wives. Isabel was different; she was quiet and studious, with a master's in art history, and several monographs on medieval art to her name. He seemed smitten with her, and I think that's why he was so reserved when he spoke about her, as opposed to his trophy wives."

"So what happened to their marriage?" Jim asked.

"Divorce, like the others."

"But why? It sounds like Isabel was a person for the long haul."

"That I don't know. One didn't have to be close to Stan to know his self-image, but details of his life I don't know. I do know that Isabel filed for divorce, not Stan. The only one of the three wives to initiate the process."

"Is Isabel still alive?"

"Yes, and I just talked to her. That's what prompted me to call you."

"Whoa, back up. Did she ask you to call me?"

"Not in so many words. But she'll be willing to talk, I'm pretty sure."

"How can I reach her?"

The caller gave Jim her number. "But let me prep her first. I'll get back in touch."

"Okay, I thank you. At least I think I do."

A rueful chuckle from the caller. "You may regret my call. I'll leave that to you to decide."

Jim was at The Long Gone when the anonymous caller reached him the next day.

Jim held the phone to his ear as he went outside to take the call.

"Go ahead, I'm listening."

"I spoke to Isabel. She's okay with talking to you. Do you have the number I gave you?"

"Yes."

"You're on your own." The caller clicked off.

Jim didn't go back inside. Instinctively he walked in the direction of the courthouse and Ted Conover's office. As he walked, phone to his ear, the #69 bus roared by headed for Harvard Square. Jim could hop on, go home, and be done with this whole messy business. Instead, he dialed Isabel's number.

"Hello?" A woman's voice. Timid in tone. Eager to talk.

"This is Judge Randall. I was given your number by someone who said you wanted to talk."

"My name is Isabel. Can we meet?"

"I would like that. Tell me where and when."

"Do you know the pizza place on Route 2?"

"No."

"Just before the prison, west of Concord."

"Okay, I know it. Has a large parking lot just off the road?"

"That's it. Can you be there this afternoon?"

Route 2 was the road Jim took when he drove to Vermont, so he knew it well. He had passed the pizza restaurant so many times he had ceased to see it. A large, standalone building at a bend in the road. The parking lot was almost empty when Jim arrived. Jim parked beside the building and entered.

There were a smattering of people at the booths and tables, and one solo woman sitting with her back to the side window. She gave Jim a tentative wave and he approached.

"Isabel?"

"Yes."

She had thick auburn hair and watch-and-wait eyes.

Jim sat down across from her. "Glad to meet you."

"I hope you don't mind meeting at this out of the way place. I feel more comfortable here."

"I don't mind at all."

"No one's here during the middle of the afternoon. After I divorced Stan, I had to be careful where I was seen. He had spies everywhere."

"It sounds like an ugly divorce."

"An understatement. Stan *hated* to lose, and when I filed for divorce, he went ballistic. And he was ruthless. If I failed to wipe after I peed, he would have used that against me in court."

Jim had the impression of a woman more comfortable in an art museum than in a marriage to a private equity vulture. There was both diffidence and defiance in her manner. "Why don't you start at the beginning and tell me what prompted you to reach out to me."

Isabel took a breath. A sun-glare on the window behind her made her expression hard to see. Jim had to squint.

"I fell in love with Stan while he was married to his first wife. She and I grew up in the same neighborhood, lost contact, then met years later on a planning committee for a charitable ball. When Stan left her for me, I felt mortified, but I couldn't help myself. Stan was very seductive then, as hard as that may be to believe. He was used to getting his way, and that can be very appealing to a self-conscious woman like me. It would be wrong to say he swept me off my feet, I threw myself at him. But only after he lowered my defenses – he was brilliant at that."

She paused and turned her head enough to see sideways out the window. When she had gathered her thoughts, she turned back to face Jim.

"Judge Randall, from what you have learned about Stan, do you consider him capable of murder?"

"I don't know enough about him to form an opinion. What's yours?"

"Yes, I believe he was."

"Explain."

"I can't prove this, but I firmly believe he tried to poison me. When I broached the subject of divorce, he seemed stricken, then he grew preternaturally calm and stayed calm even when I raised the subject again. But I started to feel unwell, not sick exactly, just unwell, as if something dangerous was happening with my body. I went to see my doctor, but she couldn't find anything wrong and speculated that the feeling was caused by the stress of my failing marriage. But my feeling of unease grew and grew and I became morbidly afraid. So I left Stan, got out of the house before he had a chance to stop me. I stayed with a friend I hadn't seen for years. I got word afterwards that Stan had hired a private detective to find me."

"Did he succeed?"

"No. I didn't see him again until I saw him in court for our divorce. By then, the ill effects of the poison had worn off, and I felt fine. Thank God I got out when I could. Stan would stop at nothing to get his way."

"Are you aware that another man died the same week as your ex-husband, a man named Arthur Maplewood?"

"Yes. And I know that Stan was trying to acquire Maplewood Naturals."

"Are you aware that Arthur Maplewood had filed a complaint against Stan with the Massachusetts attorney general?"

"I didn't know that."

"Yes. Arthur Maplewood was fighting your ex-husband's takeover attempt and had filed an ethics complaint against him."

"That's two reasons for Stan to hate him."

"In your opinion, how far would your ex-husband go when someone like Arthur Maplewood stood in his way?"

"He tried to poison me when I wanted a divorce. Business was more important to Stan than marriage. How far do *you* think Stan would go to get Arthur Maplewood out of his way?"

*

"So Stan Mitchell had motive to kill Arthur Maplewood, and Arthur Maplewood had motive to kill Stan Mitchell. Have we got two murders for the price of one?" Jim mused out loud. He and Pat were in bed, about to turn off the light.

"Or two deaths from natural causes," Pat answered.

"Or Mitchell committing suicide in front of an audience and taking his enemy Maplewood with him."

"The possibilities are endless."

"Your tone is droll," he said. "Do you think I'm tying myself into knots?"

"You? Knots? Never. But the longer I'm with you the more I appreciate your madcap imagination. Goodnight, Jim." She turned out the light.

Jim rolled onto his side facing away from Pat.

Silence.

In the dark, Jim's voice sounded amplified. "Until proven otherwise, I'll stick to my original premise, that Mitchell's death was suicide and Maplewood's from natural causes."

Pat sat up and switched on the light. "I knew it."

"Knew what?"

"That you weren't done."

Jim was on a roll. "No murders, just suicide by a man with an insatiable ego and the coincidental timing of mortal enemies dying within hours of each other."

She hesitated. "You sure?"

"No. I need a murder, any murder. At least one. I'll take two, but one is enough. I don't want to be greedy."

She turned out the light. "Goodnight, Jim."

Jim in the dark, a moment later. "We need to find out more about Maplewood, the man. He and Mitchell seem like opposites in temperament and reputation, but both were driven and both had explosive tempers. Was their hatred born of seeing themselves in each other?"

Pat groaned. "Go to sleep."

6

Arthur Maplewood had died a widower. His son, Donald, was an organic farmer in Vermont; his daughter, Vanessa, a fashion designer in New York.

Donald sounded puzzled on the phone but agreed to meet. Which gave Jim an excuse to drive to Vermont – not that he needed an excuse.

Donald's farm was across state from Jim's hillside home. A beautiful drive in green summers, multi-hued falls, and white-on-white winters; a monotonous drive through tired brown in the runt season that was Vermont in the spring. Donald Maplewood's farm on flat land near the New York border seemed removed from the rest of Vermont.

Arthur Maplewood had been a tall man, so it was a bit of a surprise to find that his son, Donald, only reached Jim's shoulders. His rimless glasses and aesthetic features belonged to a man more comfortable doing research in the stacks of a library than to a farmer, but his overalls and mud boots belonged to a man used to mucking. Donald wiped his hand before shaking Jim's. "It must be important if you came all this way."

"Not that far for me. I have a house north of Brattleboro." They were talking on the edge of a field close to the house.

"Don't know that side of the state. Dad got me a summer job near here when I was in high school, and I took to the area. I graduated from Green Mountain College and have stayed here since."

"It's your dad I want to talk about."

"You said over the phone."

"Right. I'm investigating the near-simultaneous deaths of your dad and Stan Mitchell. I don't want to upset you, but I have to consider all possibilities, including murder."

Donald didn't seem upset to hear that. "This seems like an indoors conversation. Let's go inside and I'll make some tea."

Donald dumped his boots in the mud room, which led into the kitchen. The kitchen was immaculate.

"Molly, my wife, teaches fifth and sixth grades at the local school," Donald said, leading the way to the table. "Loves it and is very good at it. Take a seat while I make some tea."

Jim sat. He could see the sky out the window above the sink. "Is your kitchen always this tidy?"

Donald let out a chuckle. "That's Molly. Sometimes I move things around for fun and watch her freak out. I tell her, 'look out the window, we live on a farm, I traffic in dirt.' She gets the joke but answers in all seriousness that's why she has to keep the house so clean."

"Makes sense."

The kettle started to boil.

In a minute, Donald brought two cups of tea to the table, and sat down. "Are you saying you think Dad killed Stan Mitchell?"

"I haven't reached any conclusions. I'm considering all possibilities. From what I've learned so far, your dad was slow to anger, but fierce when provoked."

"Yes, but to think he could be angry enough to murder is ludicrous. There's no doubt he hated Stan Mitchell –

he would've hated anyone who tried to take Maplewood Naturals away from him – but it didn't get personal until Mitchell persisted. That made Dad furious, more furious than I had ever seen him."

"Maplewood Naturals was a public company, listed on the New York Stock Exchange. Takeover attempts happen," Jim said.

"Yes. But Dad had structured the stock offering to make it unlikely he would lose control of the company. Unfortunately, Mitchell knew all the tricks. But Dad's hatred of Mitchell went beyond that. Something about Mitchell as a person infuriated Dad. I don't know what it was, maybe his utter callousness. Dad had a heart, Mitchell did not."

"You originally went into your father's line of work."

"Yes, I admired Dad and wanted to be like him. But I fell in love with farming at Green Mountain College. Farming appeals to me because the work is literally down-to-earth, which is what I wanted. No office work for me. I admired Dad and was inspired by his pioneering work in broadening organic food's appeal, but I didn't want to follow in his footsteps. When he offered me the chance to be next in line to run his company, I politely declined. He was unhappy with me for a while, but he eventually accepted my decision."

"Were you close to him?"

"Not close in the sense of sharing a lot of personal stuff. I admired him, and for the most part he admired me, but we weren't buddies."

"Did he share with you that he had filed a complaint against Mitchell with the Massachusetts attorney general?"

Donald hesitated. He turned his chair so he could see out the window.

"Yes."

"So you knew about that?"

"Yes."

"Can you tell me what was in the complaint?"

"No."

"No, you can't, or no you won't?"

"No, as in, it's none of your business."

Jim nodded. "Fair enough. Can you at least tell me this, did it have to do with Mitchell's takeover attempt?"

"More personal than that."

"His marriage?"

Donald stood. "More tea?"

"Yes, please."

Donald took the kettle from the stove and refilled Jim's cup.

"I'll say this, and I hope you understand. I don't know why you're focusing on my father's anger when you should be focusing on Mitchell's."

"Stan and I were classmates in law school. I knew Stan, I didn't know your father. That's the reason."

"Then you know."

"That Stan Mitchell specialized in pissing people off? I sure do. But what are you specifically implying?"

"Finish your tea. I've got to get back to the fields."

"I'm done. I'll walk out with you."

They paused in the mud room so Donald could put his boots on. Jim spoke as they walked out the door. "Was your father a demanding dad?"

"He set high standards."

"Standards that you could meet?"

Donald didn't break stride. "What are you getting at? Are you asking, was Dad a bully? Well, I'll tell you. He believed in completing one's job, telling the truth, not letting others down, and expected us to do the same. Is that wrong?"

"Of course not. Were you ever afraid of him?"

Donald walked several paces before responding. "No. Well, maybe sometimes. I didn't want to incur his disfavor. Aren't all sons afraid of their dads sometimes? But he was a gentle man by nature."

They walked the rest of the way in silence and stopped at the edge of a field abutting thick woods. The house was still in sight.

Jim's eyes wandered from sky to field to greenhouses and driveways. The farm seemed like Busytown compared to the hills surrounding it.

"One more question," Jim said after a moment. "Did the feud between your father and Stan Mitchell ever get out of hand?"

"Not to my knowledge. What I do know is that once my father was outraged, he stayed outraged. No forgive and forget with Dad. So, in answer to your question, the feud, as you put it, stayed hot, but as far as I know, never got out of hand."

"You have been very helpful. I realize your dad's death was a few short weeks ago, and I hope I haven't stirred up too many painful memories."

"Farming teaches equanimity. It takes a lot to rattle me."

Jim left Donald in the fields and walked back to his car. Running through Jim's mind was the question: if I had been raised on a farm, would I have become a farmer? If he asked Pat her opinion, she would probably say something like, "I can see you as a ballet dancer more readily than I can see you as a farmer."

The thought diverted Jim's mind from murder. A bulky six-footer with lead feet; a ballet dancer. I missed my calling.

When he reached his car, he turned to look at the field he had come from. Donald Maplewood was a stick figure silhouetted against a stand of trees and an overarching sky.

Jim climbed in his car and headed across state. Murder by Maplewood seemed improbable. The founder of Maplewood Naturals? The organic foods maestro with an even disposition and an aesthetic son?

How about murder by Mitchell? Mitchell had a temper and was used to bullying his way to his goals. But why would he murder when he was so close to death himself? Jim remembered how withered he looked at the dinner in his honor the night he died.

Jim stopped for a bite along the way and got to his house at dusk. The first thing he did was call Pat.

"I'm back at the house. How are you?"

"Busy."

"Oh?"

"Re-reading my cases for the *Bench Life* sequel."

"Let me ask you, do you think I'd be a good farmer?"

Pat laughed. "Probably the best ever."

"Or maybe a ballet dancer. What do you think? Would I look good in tights?"

"Tights? Jim, are you okay?"

"I just got back from Donald Maplewood's farm. I read him as a dreamer who has shoehorned his dreams into organic farming. If his father hadn't built a company based on organic foods, my guess is Donald would have found some other way of life than farming. I can see him teaching eastern philosophy and religion at a small liberal arts college. He doesn't quite fit the life he has chosen."

"Are you any closer to knowing who dun it?"

"No. But I never know what tidbits I glean along the way will lead me to the answer, until I find the answer."

"When do you think you'll come home?"

"When my thoughts have jelled. Another day or two."

"Good. Come to think of it, you'd look adorable in toe shoes."

Jim stayed another day, then drove home. He felt adrift once home. Even the live poultry shop and Beauty Shop Row failed to anchor him: too many possibilities, too few answers. He hated this stage of an investigation.

What was he missing? Since the week of the dual deaths, he had the nagging feeling there was a clue lying just beyond his reach. A nudge, a jolt, that would point him in the right direction. He knew from experience that when he found it, it would seem so obvious he'd wonder how he could have missed it.

Then Jim remembered the last words he heard Stan Mitchell say: "Don't believe your eyes."

What could Stan have meant? It seemed portentous at the time but more likely was something mundane. Was the comment even directed at Jim? Maybe it was meant for one of the other well-wishers who were crowding Stan at the time. Or maybe Jim's nagging feeling of something missing had nothing to do with what Mitchell said, maybe it had to do with the thought in the back of Jim's head that refused to come out of hiding.

After checking his mail and washing the clothes he wore in Vermont, he went to Pat's for the night. They ate dinner in the bistro at the base of Beacon Hill. Pat sat with her back to the window.

"I'm overlooking something," Jim said as he scanned the menu, which he knew by heart; the bistro was not Duck, Duck, Goose, but it would do. "It bothered me the whole drive home."

"That's one difference between you and me. You brood."

Jim idly watched the pedestrians passing the window. "Sorry, what did you say?"

"I asked, what are you going to eat?"

"Steak frites. Once in a while won't kill me."

"You said you need to lower your cholesterol."

"Don't nag me, please."

"I don't need to nag. I just stare at people like this." Pat's eyes darkened and her lips tightened, and whoever was in her line of sight turned to ash.

Jim laughed. "Be that as it may, I remain haunted by the histories of Mitchell and Maplewood. The near simultaneous deaths of two men who hated each other can't be a coincidence, can it? I know from experience that coincidences do happen, but rarely this extreme."

Their food arrived.

"Is your steak cooked the way you like it?" Pat asked, as Jim cut into his.

"Just right."

They ate silently for several minutes. Jim broke the silence by changing the subject.

"As you review your cases for your memoir, are there any you regret? Verdicts you think were wrong?"

"Do you ask for a reason?"

"Because you were a good judge and you are examining your past. I'm curious what you are learning."

Pat put down her fork. "One case of mine still gives me the chills, a murder case where I got hopelessly tangled in clues and totally missed the salient point. Only a good defense attorney saved me from giving the jury misleading and prejudicial instructions. The murder turned out to be suicide. I shudder to think how close I came to sending an innocent man to prison."

"How will you handle that in your memoir?"

"The same way I handled my mistakes in *Bench Life*. I'll admit them but won't wallow in them. Mea culpa but not mega-mea culpa. Excessive self-flagellation strikes me as akin to self-pity. You are guilty of that sometimes." She hesitated. "Why are you staring at me like that?"

Jim shook his head. "I'm glad I was never on trial in your courtroom. I'd plead guilty solely to escape your withering gaze."

"So you'll defer to me from now on?"

"Not a chance. Remember, in the bedroom I'm boss." His eyes came close to twinkling.

She guffawed so loudly Jim turned to see if anyone had noticed. Apparently not.

They walked uphill after dinner. The night was clear. Even with a full moon and the occasional street lamp, the uneven brick sidewalks of Beacon Hill were an obstacle course, and halfway up, Pat tripped. Jim reached out and steadied her before she could fall.

"Okay?" he said.

"Yes. You'd think I'd know these sidewalks by now."

He kept his hand on her elbow as they walked. "Do you feel like coming with me to New York?"

"You're going to New York?"

"Yes, to visit Vanessa Maplewood. Donald was helpful, but he wouldn't tell me everything I wanted to know. Maybe his sister will be more forthcoming."

7

The 9:10 a.m. Amtrak to New York was full as usual. Jim took the window seat, Pat the aisle.

"Where are we meeting Vanessa?" Pat asked as the train skirted the Connecticut coastline.

"Her office."

"I've never been in a fashion designer's office," Pat said.

"Oh, I have. Many times."

"To order your high-fashion judicial robes, I presume?"

"You nailed it."

The coastline was studded with inlets and bays, cubbyholes for the rising light that bounced off the water. Jim felt eternal watching, which was ironic given the ever-changing nature of sand and sunlight.

He glanced at Pat to see if she, too, were looking out the window. She was.

"This view never gets old," he said.

"Makes one feel insignificant, doesn't it?"

The power plants and playing fields on the cusp of Manhattan brought them back to earth with a thud. As the train approached the city, it detoured over a crumbling railroad bridge into Long Island, lumbered above the row houses and auto repair shops of Queens, then looped back towards Manhattan before ducking into the tunnel to Penn Station.

Pat had booked a hotel room between the station and the Garment District. They checked their bags at the front desk and got a bite to eat at a diner. Vanessa's office was within walking distance.

It felt good to walk after three and a half hours on the train (Amtrak Acela – the high-speed train that couldn't). The Garment District was dingy, noisy, and not at all chic, which made the fact that it was home to the fashion industry all the more chic.

Vanessa's office was businesslike. Vanessa was too. She strode into her outer office with outstretched hand, a running back stiff-arming a tackler, and shook Pat and Jim's hands with vigor. No time to waste, her handshake said. She was no-nonsense pretty, unpretentiously stylish. "Come into my office," she gestured at her glass walled inner sanctum.

She started talking before she sat. "You are here because of my father. You should know at the start that he and I were affectionate but not close. What can I do for you?"

Pat took the lead. "We're sorry for your loss. To lose a father is hard, whether or not your relationship was close."

Vanessa studied Pat. "Yes."

"Jim and I were judges on the same court. Now that we're both retired, we occasionally collaborate on puzzles like why your father and Stan Mitchell died within hours of each other after feuding for years. We have no official role. We're curious by nature and we know our way around the legal system, so sometimes we can be of help to law enforcement. Did your father ever confide in you about his feud with Stan Mitchell?"

"Never. Didn't even acknowledge it," Vanessa answered.

"He never expressed an opinion about Mitchell?"

"He had no use for Stan Mitchell, that was no secret. But confide in me? Never."

Jim took up the questioning. "How often did you see your father?"

"Two or three times a year. My brother and I would visit him in Boston and talk about how much we missed Mom. Dad especially missed her. He had a permanent air of melancholy after she died."

"Nobody took her place?"

"Dad was loyal, perhaps to a fault. He was incapable of transferring his affections from Mom to another woman, and he was equally loyal to his employees. Dad didn't go to college, and maybe because of that had great respect for the value of hard work. He repeatedly told Donald and me that all work has dignity."

"He sounds like a fine man."

Vanessa became animated. "Yes, he was, but make no mistake, he was a formidable foe. Dad was gentle and kind but tougher than nails. I'm sure Stan Mitchell didn't expect the pushback he got."

"Your dad had filed an ethics complaint against Mitchell with the Masschusetts Attorney General before he died. Did he ever mention it?"

"Never. I saw Dad two months before he died, and he said nothing. I was surprised to find him unusually reflective, almost wistful, as if forces he couldn't control had been unleashed. Could the ethics complaint have something to do with that?"

"Could be. Did he seem frightened for his safety?"

"Not his safety, per se, apprehensive about what might come next. Wait, I just remembered, Dad mentioned that an ex-wife of Stan Mitchell's had asked to meet with him. Dad seemed uncomfortable with the idea."

"Did he mention her name?"

"Isabel, I think. I don't know if she and Dad ever met. Strange timing, when I think about it now. And now I have to go. I hate when anyone is late to a meeting, and I will be late to one if I don't leave now." She extended her hand.

"You've been very helpful," Jim said, shaking her hand.

"Yes, we thank you very much," Pat echoed.

"Please let me know if you learn anything about Dad's death."

"We will. And thanks again."

The noise of the city precluded conversation when Pat and Jim reached the sidewalk. They started walking.

"What was she telling us?" Pat said when the noise briefly abated.

"That her father was apprehensive near the end of his life, and that his ethics complaint against Stan Mitchell may only be partly why."

Pat nodded. "Next question, did Isabel have information about her ex-husband she wanted Arthur Maplewood to know? Is that why she requested a meeting?"

"And if so, what could it be?" Jim said. "Something about the takeover attempt? Remember, Maplewood owned a controlling share of the company, so the only way Stan Mitchell could acquire the company was by persuading Maplewood to sell. Maybe Mitchell was strong-arming the other stockholders to put pressure on Maplewood. Maybe Maplewood's ethics complaint had to do with the tactics Mitchell was using to pressure the other stockholders."

They stopped on the curb of a busy intersection. A taxi dodging a delivery van brushed them back, its air-blast teeter-tottering them.

The walk light came on. They started across.

"Isabel didn't share any of this when I met with her," Jim said. "I wonder why?"

"Meet with her again."

"My thought exactly," Jim said as they mounted the curb on the other side of the street.

*

The parking lot of the pizza place on Route 2 was as empty as the first time Jim met Isabel there. How did it stay in business, Jim wondered as he parked his car and headed into the restaurant.

Isabel was sitting at the same table, backlit as before.

Jim pulled out the chair across the table. "How are you?"

"Fine. Why did you ask to see me again?"

"Coffee," he said over his shoulder to the woman who came to take their order. "Pat and I met with Arthur Maplewood's daughter, Vanessa, in New York yesterday. She said you asked to see her father a few months before his death. She didn't know why. Can you tell me?"

"I wanted Arthur to know that Stan had tried to poison me when I told him I was leaving him. I worried what he might do in order to acquire Maplewood Naturals."

"You thought Stan might murder Arthur Maplewood?"

"I wanted Arthur to know the lengths Stan would go to when he wanted something badly enough. Arthur seemed startled."

Jim had a hunch. "Had you known Arthur before you married Stan?"

Isabel hesitated slightly. "Yes."

"Care to tell me about it?"

"When I was in business school he taught a mini-course on branding a business. He was a dozen years older and not my type, but he was passionate about organic foods, evangelical about them, which I found very seductive. He was unmarried at the time. We had a brief but intense romance."

"This was before you married Stan Mitchell? Did Mitchell know about you and Maplewood?"

"I told him when I filed for divorce, which was a mistake because Stan couldn't fathom that I might be divorcing him because he was an asshole. When he learned about my early relationship with Arthur, he assumed I still carried a flame for him, or worse, had hooked up with him again, and that was the reason I was divorcing him, which wasn't true."

"Do you think your affair played any role in Stan's takeover attempt of Arthur's company?"

"I do. Stan was insanely jealous of anyone he perceived as better at business or love than he. A competitor who built a successful company and became a symbol for a new category of food violated Stan's king-of-the-hill mentality. Stan's first and foremost interest was business, but his manhood wasn't far behind. And when..." A couple sat down two tables away, which momentarily distracted Isabel. "When Arthur filed his ethics complaint against Mitchell, it must have been the last straw. The former lover of the woman who divorced you files an ethics complaint against your business practices – it must have driven Stan insane."

*

The Route 2 traffic was rush-hour heavy by the time Jim left the restaurant. He avoided the traffic by taking a side road not knowing where it led, which could pose a problem because his sense of direction was not unerring. Oh, well, he thought, the woods and housing developments are pretty. He used the meandering time to put himself in Stan Mitchell's head. Isabel had painted Stan as a thin-skinned narcissist who had to be the dominant person in any scenario. Imagine yourself as Mitchell, Jim told himself. Old, sick, dissed. As he did, he could feel his ire rising, his outrage growing. Retaliate, retaliate, he heard in his head, but against whom? No matter. Hurt somebody, anybody.

Jim shook his head to rid it of Mitchell. Even with twenty-plus years of observing humanity from the bench, Jim didn't understand people who insisted on always being the biggest, the best, the first.

Maybe Mitchell wasn't that awful – Jim was only imagining himself into Mitchell's head, after all – but he wouldn't bet on it. If he had to, he'd bet that Stan Mitchell remained the jerk he had been in law school, raised to the nth power.

Jim found himself on a road beside a stream. No other cars were on the road and he suddenly had the feeling he would never find his way home, that the road would get narrower and narrower until it and he turned to dust.

Mitchell is getting to you, Jim. Step back, take a breath.

That night Jim and Pat ate at Duck, Duck, Goose, their local favorite. Bruce, at the front desk, plucked two menus from the top of a pile and showed Jim and Pat to their table. "Where have you been? We've missed you."

"It hasn't been that long," Jim protested.

"Tonight we have a pork chop you wouldn't believe," Bruce said, depositing the menus on the table. "And you have to try the Meyer lemon semifreddo for dessert."

"I don't think so," Jim replied, remembering a mistake he had made in another case.

Bruce gave a breezy, "Enjoy."

"Wine, I need wine," Jim said, scanning the list to see if it contained anything new.

"You said you'd tell me about your meeting with Isabel."

"Wine first."

A bottle of Gigondas was presented and poured.

"Isabel was involved with Arthur Maplewood before she married Stan Mitchell."

"I wondered."

"Did you? Why didn't you say something?"

"Because I wasn't sure it would make any difference," Pat said.

"Isabel doesn't think jealousy was the deciding factor in Mitchell trying to take over Maplewood's business, but it may have contributed. Apparently Mitchell was unable to accept anybody beating him in sex or business. I came away rooting for Arthur Maplewood to have murdered him."

"You're in danger of becoming too caught up in this, Jim. You can't bring either man back to life."

"In Stan Mitchell's case that's probably a good thing. But I find myself unable to let it go."

They didn't talk about the case again until they were walking home. The night felt soft. "Why do I keep doing this? I'm very happy with you, I read and brood to my heart's content, I walk whenever I want, I love my house in Vermont, yet I can't stop rubbing shoulders with murderers."

"Know thyself, Jim."

"What if I don't like what I find?"

"Then hide behind your ego like Stan Mitchell."

Jim unlocked the door to his townhouse and they climbed the stairs to the bedroom.

"The Mitchell-Maplewood murders have everything – sex, jealousy, ego, money, business reputations – everything except murder," Jim said as they got ready for bed.

"Exactly. Which is why you can't let it go."

Jim looked at Pat, regal even in pajamas.

"Am I making a fool of myself?"

"Not at all. I find your obsessiveness endearing."

"But in the eyes of the rest of the world?"

"Jim, the rest of the world isn't looking."

Flat on his back in the dark, Jim felt like a boy again. He remembered how bewildered he felt as a boy, how he had to rely on a father he didn't have much faith in and who died too early. Not that Jim's father was cruel – he could be stark in his warnings: the world is a treacherous place, protect yourself at all times, etc. – but not cruel. Basically his father was well-intentioned but ill-equipped. As a result, Jim developed self-reliance early on, which left him insular, maybe to a fault. Yet being self-reliant was not a bad quality for a judge, who had to make decision after decision on his own.

He lay on his back wondering how to prove there was at least one murder the night Mitchell and Maplewood died. He didn't want this to be the first case to stump him.

8

As a plain-and-simple eater, Jim knew little about organic food. He thought it meant food grown without the use of pesticides, that's all he knew. But every subcategory of food develops its own vocabulary and its own ideology, which in some cases approaches the religious. Adherents became zealots, zealots became fanatics. He never understood that impulse: why complicate life with rigid rules and zealotry? The middle, the golden mean, moderation in all things, except amateur sleuthing. There zealotry is called for.

The question Jim faced was, what were the business reasons Stan Mitchell was so intent on acquiring Maplewood Naturals? He understood the ego-driven, insecurity-fueled reasons, but what were the business reasons?

Mitchell's private equity firm was basically Stan Mitchell and Glen Hudson, his longtime partner, a man content to let Stan Mitchell be the face of the company. Mitchell's name often appeared in the business press; Glen Hudson's name rarely.

Hudson reluctantly agreed to meet with Jim. He sounded curious rather than eager and when he shook hands with Jim in his State Street office, he seemed even less eager than over the phone.

"Have a seat."

Fifties, dapper, slicked-back hair glistening like newly poured asphalt. If looks could sneer. He settled into a leather chair and waited.

"Thanks for meeting with me," Jim began.

"What do you want, Judge Randall? Why are you here?"

Don't waste my time, Hudson's tone said. So Jim didn't.

"Why did your boss want to acquire Maplewood Naturals?"

"A lot of people feared Stan, but he was a good boss and he suffered terribly at the end of his life. Now that he's gone, his haters have come out of hiding. I have no patience for them."

"You didn't answer my question. From a purely business perspective, was Maplewood Naturals an obvious takeover target for your firm?"

"No, very unusual. Most companies we pursued were in financial trouble and would go out of business if we didn't snatch them up, whereas Maplewood Naturals was thriving. I was surprised when Stan told me he was pursuing it. But after he explained his reasoning, the acquisition made sense. Stan had decided that organic foods were the next big thing in the grocery business. He predicted that every major grocery chain soon would be carrying organic foods, not just the Whole Foods of the world. Food is one of the essential human needs. The organic food fad might fade, but the demand for food never would. Organic food was Stan's way into the broader food market."

"Compelling. Did you get on board immediately?"

"No. We didn't go after thriving companies – the risk of losing was too great. But when I stopped to think about the advantages of having a foothold in the food business to tide us over the vicissitudes of the bankruptcy market, I became a convert."

"Where does the takeover attempt stand now?"

"After Stan's death, the steam went out of it. I'm officially still trying, but I'm not pushing too hard."

"So Stan's death was good for Maplewood Naturals?"

"I suppose so. I hadn't thought of it that way. You don't think...You're not saying...."

"I'm not saying anything. I'm here to learn."

"I have to admit that both men dying within a week of each other gave me pause. But murder? Stan and I were professional vultures. We fed on dead carcasses, so I'm not squeamish, but offing one's competitors seems a little extreme, even to a vulture."

Hudson was a little less curt by the time he ushered Jim out of his office a quarter hour later. One small step for mankind. Jim stood on the sidewalk and took stock. The building he had just emerged from was an anonymous stone office building leftover from Boston's glory days. Boston had been a commercial hub when shipping reigned supreme and Boston was the closest port to Europe. Now Boston was an education and health care hub, and Cambridge across the river – home of MIT and Harvard – was rapidly becoming Silicon Valley East.

He stood wondering what it was like to live and die by the deal as Stan Mitchell had done; you needed a certain temperament – a temperament he, Jim, certainly didn't have. He liked to ponder, to cogitate, then pronounce, not gamble and pounce.

A judicial bench had been the right place for him. So what was he doing, standing outside the offices of a firm that took chances on failing companies, wondering who killed whom?

He walked to a nearby lunch place he knew. He sat on a stool and scanned a menu. Old fashioned food only. His kind of food. Come to papa.

The financial district is a short walk from Beacon Hill, so after lunch – feeling bloated and unhealthy but happy – he walked the few blocks to Pat's.

Pat was working on the second installment of her memoir.

She looked up from her writing desk. She wrote in a corner of her living room near the open dining area.

"How was it?"

Jim rarely resorted to whimsey because it didn't come naturally to him, but sometimes it came in handy. "I'm a new man."

"How so?"

"I've become a risk taker, a trendsetter. Can't you tell?"

Solemnly, she nodded. "Absolutely. It's written all over you."

He paced. "I'm missing something important. I don't know what it is."

"We've changed the subject, have we?"

"I'm serious. What have I overlooked?"

She stood from her writing desk and took Jim by the arm. "Don't obsess, Jim, that's when your brain locks up. Relax, let go. It'll come to you."

He wanted to brainstorm with Ted Conover. Ted could squeeze Jim in for an early morning breakfast the next day.

Usually Jim would walk to Ted's, but it was raining when he woke up, so he took the T instead. The early morning commuters seemed listless, but it was the listlessness of not loving what one was heading to rather than the listlessness of depletion, of being spent, which was the usual mood in the afternoon. He walked from the T station to the diner where he was to meet Ted. The rain fell in batches, like carpet bombing. His umbrella did a miserable job of keeping him dry. He arrived at the diner sodden.

Ted was perched on a counter stool.

Jim sat down beside him. "Morning."

"You look like hell."

"Really?" Jim was a little stung.

"Although that may be my tired eyes. I've been on a trial treadmill, and the treadmill keeps going faster and faster. How are you?"

"Fine, until you told me I look like hell."

Ted smiled. "Jim, you always look like hell."

Ted was eating bacon and eggs. Jim ordered oatmeal and wheat toast.

"Coffee?" the pleasant woman behind the counter asked, coffee pot at the ready.

"Please. And plenty of it."

When she had gone, Jim explained his current thinking about Mitchell and Maplewood. "What am I missing? What do you hear when I talk about their deaths?"

"Maplewood seems like a nice guy, Mitchell does not, so one hopes Mitchell is the bad guy. But we both know of cases of good guys pushed beyond their limit doing bad things. Let's compare motives: Maplewood – to prevent Mitchell from acquiring his company. Mitchell – to get Maplewood out of the way so he could acquire Maplewood's company, to feed his ego, and to thwart a potentially embarrassing outcome of an ethics complaint. So I'd go with Mitchell as having more motive."

"Me too. We have plenty of motive. All we need now is a murder."

*

As he drove to Donald Maplewood's organic farm, Jim wasn't concerned that he didn't have a plan in mind, having become more comfortable with winging life and law since he left the bench. And when he found himself standing in what he guessed was a lettuce field – although it could be kale, or beets, or spinach; he actually had no idea – asking Donald Maplewood if he would agree to exhuming his father's body, he wasn't surprised the plan came to him when he needed it.

A look of extreme incredulity spread over Donald's face.

"You've got to be kidding. We buried him only a few weeks ago, and now you want us to dig him up and cut him open?"

"I understand why my request shocks you. I'd feel the same way if it were my father. But there are questions only a thorough autopsy can answer."

The sun shone over Donald's shoulder forcing Jim to squint.

"I liked you when we met, felt sympathy for you and what you were doing, but now...." Donald hesitated. "The answer is no. NO. Have you asked my sister?"

"I have not."

"I dare you. She'll tear your head off. Let's go in the house."

The soil felt spongy under Jim's feet. The air smelled pungent.

"Can you feel the land we're walking on? I get immense gratification out of working it. I can understand how you get gratification out of playing detective, but what you are asking me to authorize is not an abstract matter to me. Dad deserves to rest in peace. Dig him up? Cut him open? Are you kidding?"

They reached the house. A tea kettle was on the stove when they entered. "Have a seat. Tea?"

"Please."

"I want to be reasonable. If there are things about Dad's death my sister and I should know, I'd like to help." He put a cup of tea on the kitchen table in front of Jim. "Where are you going with this? What do you expect to find?"

"I don't expect to find anything in particular. But your dad and Stan Mitchell were enemies, and they died in the same week, so I'd like to know one way or the other whether either was murdered – or both."

"Dad died from cardiac-related complications of diabetes, according to his doctor. Dad had suffered heart problems for years, so I wasn't surprised by his death. Shocked when it happened, but not entirely surprised."

"Did you notice any unusual changes in his heath during his final weeks?"

"Yes, his energy dropped off a cliff. Sometimes he lacked the strength to speak. I begged him to see his doctor, but he resisted. Dad could be stubborn to a fault. What are you suggesting?"

"It could be related to heart problems, but there are poisons that are hard to trace when given in small doses over a period of time, and the person being poisoned usually doesn't realize what is happening. I'm not saying poison is what killed your father, but an autopsy could rule that out. Did Stan Mitchell have contact with your father in the weeks before their deaths?"

"Not Mitchell. His business associate, Glen Hudson, met with Dad several times before Dad's death."

"Had they come to an agreement?"

"To the contrary, Dad said they were further apart than ever. I remember my dad at the time muttering he'd like to kill Mitchell. I didn't take him seriously."

"Would you give me permission to talk to your father's lawyer?"

"I'd have to clear it with Vanessa."

"She's the boss?"

"She has business sense I lack. Dad wanted to leave his company to her, but she wasn't interested. If Vanessa okays you talking to Dad's lawyer, it's okay with me."

Jim sat in his car for a moment before driving off. He was on to something; he didn't know quite what, but it signaled to Jim: keep going.

He drove south towards Bennington where he would pick up the cross-state road to Brattleboro. He liked this corner of Vermont, didn't get here often. On a whim, he turned west instead of east at Bennington, seeking to cross a border, the border here being that between Vermont and New York. He liked the landforms on the other side, so different than those of Vermont. The Hudson River and ice age glaciers had done their work, leaving the land craggy, grooved, and unpredictable. Flat land? Ridged land? Tongue-and-groove land? All of the above. It was as if the maker of the universe had thrown up his or her hands at the sight of so many impending geological collisions and cried, "Go for it!"

He liked land that mirrored his mental state, and given his current indecision, the cross-hatched land suited him perfectly. He pulled off to the side of the road and called Vanessa.

He could envision the phone ringing in her nondescript office building in the unfashionable garment district.

"Vanessa Maplewood's office."

"This is Judge Randall. Is she there?"

"I'm sorry, Judge. She is not. May I give her a message?"

He left his number and asked that she call.

To re-cross the border was to reenter earth's atmosphere. A change in air pressure. Nonsense, of course. But why couldn't he indulge in nonsense once in a while, especially when he thought he was on to something? Staid Jim Randall on the outside, madcap Jim Randall on the inside.

Nonsense was actually a good sign in Jim's history as a sleuth. It meant he was getting closer to a solution.

The drive across state was uneventful and he reached his house in just over an hour. Vanessa called back as he parked his car in the driveway.

"Hold for Vanessa Maplewood."

"Good morning, Judge. My brother told me you'd be calling. I'm afraid my answer's the same as his. No."

"No to which question?"

"Exhuming Dad's body."

"How about the name of your father's lawyer?"

"You asked Donald for the name of Dad's attorney?"

"I did."

"He failed to mention that. Donald shares the minimum of information with me. I think he's afraid of me. He confuses me with the Meryl Streep character."

"You just lost me."

"The Devil Wears Prada. Very funny film."

"I didn't see it. I don't see many movies."

"Books. I can see you in a book-lined study reading Plato."

"Cicero."

"Even better. He was a lawyer of some renown. Are you seeking the terms of Dad's will? Is that why you want his attorney's name? I can save you the trouble. Dad's will divided his estate equally between Donald and me. But given your endless curiosity, I suspect that won't satisfy you, so his attorney's name is Matthew Jenkins. He's based in Boston. I'll tell him you'll call."

Jim waited to call until he was back in Cambridge. He called from his book-lined study, looking at the hind ends of jumbled together triple-deckers. The Connecticut River valley it was not.

"Vanessa told me you would call, Judge Randall. I know you by reputation."

"If it's not good, don't tell me."

Jenkins' voice was the voice of a senior citizen, a seasoned lawyer. "Sometimes intimidating, always fair, I hear. What can I do for you?"

"Vanessa told me her father divided his estate equally between her and her brother. Did his will leave instructions about Maplewood Naturals?"

"Since neither of his children wanted to run the company, Arthur's will instructs me to divide his shares of

Maplewood Naturals stock equally between Vanessa and Donald."

"Which would mean that Maplewood Naturals would be subject to a hostile takeover unless Vanessa and Donald joined forces to stop it."

"That's correct."

"It's sad in a way. I didn't know Arthur Maplewood, but from what I have learned, he cared deeply about his company."

"Yes, I agree. Its likely fate after the will is probated is that Maplewood Naturals will be absorbed by a conglomerate."

"Is Mitchell Equity still interested in acquiring it?"

"Technically, yes, but since Stan's death, I sense that the interest has waned."

"Can we chat in person about a delicate subject? Can you spare me a few minutes?"

"It would be my pleasure. Come to my office tomorrow at six. I will be happy to finally meet the esteemed Judge Randall."

Jenkins' office was located in the maze of streets of Boston's financial district. Glass-walled high-rises were crowding out the stately sandstone buildings but there were a few venerable buildings left. Jenkins' office was in one of them.

He was as he sounded over the phone, a man of considerable gravitas. He wore his ample weight like a well-tailored suit. "Have a seat, Judge Randall. It's good to finally meet you. Do you miss your robe?"

"More my gavel."

Jenkins had a knowing smile. "I'm nearing my firm's mandatory retirement age, and I'm starting to miss the work already. You took up solving crime, I have no such passions."

"I didn't either when I left the bench. I fell into it when my friend Ted Conover asked for my help."

"I know Ted. He's the heart and soul of the DA's office. Fine man."

"Tell me about Arthur Maplewood's final days. Vanessa said there was rapid decline in his health that was inconsistent with the gradual decline he had suffered for years. Did you notice the same thing?"

"Yes. Arthur had been declining for years, but this seemed different, as if somebody had pushed him off a cliff. I asked him what was wrong, and he claimed it was just old age, that his diabetes was under control, but I didn't believe him. He had a nurse with him 24 hours a day."

"Do you believe someone wanted him out of the way?"

"The thought crossed my mind. His decline coincided with Stan Mitchell's takeover attempt. We were not budging, and on top of that, Arthur had lodged a complaint with the attorney general about the tactics Mitchell was using. Mitchell could barely control his temper the times we met. I wasn't sure he would get out of our meetings alive. He was in terrible physical condition."

"What did the complaint allege?"

"That Stan Mitchell was hacking the computers of Maplewood Naturals, including Arthur's personal emails, trying to dig up dirt to blackmail Arthur with."

"Had he found anything, as far as you know?"

"I don't know, but I know that Arthur was evangelical about the gospel of organic foods. I suspect Mitchell intercepted the thoughts of an evangelist."

They talked for another fifteen minutes, then Jenkins said, "Judge Randall, forgive me, but I've got a museum gala to attend. I've enjoyed meeting you. If you need to talk more, I can arrange that."

"Thank you for being so helpful. One more thing: what was the name of Stan Mitchell's lawyer?"

"Susan Coyle, of Rawlins, Morrison, and Keene. Be careful. She'll charm you, then eat you alive."

The financial district was almost dark when Jim left Jenkins's office. He walked through brightly lit Downtown Crossing, then across the Common and uphill to Pat's.

"Don't take off your coat. I made a reservation at the Italian place," she said.

Jim had his coat halfway off. He slipped his arm back in the sleeve. "At your service."

The walk downhill to Charles Street was a lark compared to the trek uphill.

"Why don't you move to flat land?" Jim asked as they walked.

"I love it here."

"Me too. I'm just tired."

"And you live on flat land," she reminded him.

"That is true."

He hadn't been hungry before, but now was in the mood for pasta.

"Are you okay with Italian for a change?" she asked.

"Just what I'm in the mood for."

"How was Maplewood's lawyer?"

"Solid citizen, fine lawyer."

"Helpful?"

"To the extent he could be. Maplewood's will divided his estate equally between Donald and Vanessa, neither of whom wanted to run his company, so its likely fate was to be sold to a conglomerate."

They reached the restaurant. Jim ordered a bottle of Sangiovese, a decent wine, if not French. When the wine came, Jim offered a toast to Pat. "Now we shall enjoy our meal and go back to your place and violate each other's bodies in ways that could get us disbarred."

Pat looked bemused. "Do I have a say in the matter?"

"You can say anything you want while we're having sex, preferably 'oh my god, oh my god, oh my god!'"

*

Susan Coyle said no over the phone. She wouldn't meet with Jim. Attorney-client privilege, etc.

"Your late client," Jim corrected. "Stan Mitchell is no longer with us."

"The privilege remains. I'm sorry, Judge Randall. I argued a case in your courtroom years ago, do you remember?"

"Remind me."

"A banker accused of embezzlement. My first embezzlement case."

"I'm sorry, I don't. But that means nothing. My memory is not what it used to be, and it wasn't all that great before."

"Well, I remember you. You struck me as a model judge."

"You are kind. May I ask a last question?"

"Of course."

"Does Mitchell's private equity firm still hope to acquire Maplewood Naturals?"

"The offer is still on the table."

9

When you hit a wall after making forward progress, it feels like more of a setback than if you hadn't made any forward progress. A major setback is what it felt like now to Jim.

He had learned what he wanted to learn. He had learned the terms of Maplewood's will, he had learned the likely fate of Maplewood Naturals, he had learned something of the dynamics of the Maplewood family, and he had learned that Mitchell was an easy man to hate.

All good. All useful. But not enough.

Was anyone murdered? He still didn't know.

If either man was murdered, how could Jim find out? Each man's doctor had determined the cause of death, and in each case the cause was found to be natural, the result of disease. Jim doubted if either man's doctor would or could shed more light, assuming either doctor would be willing to talk to him, which was doubtful.

Mitchell's body had been cremated, and Maplewood's children refused to allow their father's body to be exhumed and an autopsy performed.

So Jim was stuck, the wall had been hit.

Relax, Jim, let go. He remembered Pat's words, and he thought they were wise. Easier said than done. Driving to his house in Vermont had proved the un-sticking point in the past, but it didn't feel appropriate now. The clue he was looking for was close to home. He just needed a nudge, a hint; he would take it from there.

He wandered in body and mind the next few days, taking long walks on the Esplanade or by Beauty Shop Row. The Charles River as viewed from the Esplanade was more a basin that a river, nothing like the Connecticut River as seen from his Vermont hillside home. Yet he found water soothing no matter the setting. It was as if the movement of water did some of the thinking for him. And Beauty Shop Row always made him chuckle – so many hair salons, so little time – which helped relax the mind.

Yet the walking and woolgathering did not work this time. A nudge, a clue, my kingdom for a clue. Frustrated, he gave up on Friday afternoon and headed towards Pat's aerie across the revered if crumbling Longfellow Bridge.

The river was metallic this day. At the highest point of the arched bridge, Jim paused to catch his breath. Massachusetts General Hospital, a massive fortress of health, anchored the left side of the bridge. Jim could envision the doctors, nurses, and patients hurrying through its corridors oblivious to the metallic water and stately sky.

He reached the end of the bridge. New construction amidst the already massive hospital complex caught his eye. A bulky square building with too many windows crammed into a space where it didn't fit, adding weight that wasn't needed.

Almost home. Home on this side of the bridge being Pat's. Then the nudge he had been seeking entered his mind. The hint, the clue, the jolt he needed. He quickened his pace as much as he could and made it up the hill to Pat's in record time.

"Are you okay?" she asked when he came gasping through the door.

"Out of breath, is all."

"What's wrong? Why are you in such a hurry? Jim, you need to be careful, you're not young."

He held her shoulders, dipped his head. "Coming across the bridge, I remembered Maplewood's lawyer saying that Stan Mitchell always had a nurse with him when they met. Then I remembered seeing a nurse with Mitchell at our law school reunion the night he died. I can picture the nurse wheeling him onto the stage. It made me think: given how frail he was and that he lived alone, I'll bet he had a live-in nurse."

"Okay," Pat said, quizzically.

Jim released her shoulders. "Don't you see? Maybe Mitchell unburdened himself to the nurse before he died, a death bed confession if you will, or maybe he accidentally let something slip in the nurse's presence. If you're with someone 24/7, stuff can slip out you didn't mean to say."

"Try the agencies."

"No. I'm going to try Mitchell's lawyer, Susan Coyle."

Susan Coyle had not been helpful the first time Jim called, but he was put through to her this time without trouble.

"Did Stan Mitchell have live-in nursing care in his final months?"

"Yes."

"I'd like to speak to one of the nurses who took care of him."

She thought for a minute. "You're really into this, aren't you? Fine, go for it. You won't learn anything. The Safe At Home Agency in Medford supplied the nurses. You can use my name."

*

The small city of Medford has few characteristics to distinguish it from the other small cities crowded together north of Boston: multi-family houses with no yards; a downtown with locally-owned stores, a broken-in but not broken-down kind of town. If Medford were an item of clothing, it would be a well-worn pair of jeans. An advantage from Jim's perspective was that it abuts Somerville, the next town over from Cambridge, making it easy for Jim to reach. The Safe At Home agency was located near Lawrence Hospital in the same building as the women's maternity clinic.

The receptionist had a Spanish accent and a pleasant manner.

"How may I help you?"

"I'm Judge Jim Randall. I am trying to locate the home care nurses you supplied to Stan Mitchell before he died."

The woman frowned. She didn't want to be unhelpful but she was puzzled. "May I ask why you are interested in locating the nurses?"

"Yes, because I am investigating Mr. Mitchell's death."

"And you said you are a judge?"

"Retired. Now I'm a free-lance sleuth. Susan Coyle, Mr. Mitchell's attorney, gave me your agency's name."

The woman reached for her phone. "I need to get our director's okay."

A muted conversation, then Jim was told the director was out but would be back in an hour.

"You can try her then. Linda Gomez-Martin. Her office is on the second floor."

"You've been very helpful. I realize my request is unorthodox."

"We have to be careful. So much hatred today, and with the women's maternity clinic next door, we get a lot of spillover anger."

Jim wandered towards what he thought was downtown but which brought him to the river. The Mystic, not the Charles. The Mystic was not majestic but water was water, and Jim walked beside it as long as there was a path. He hadn't looked to see what time he left the Safe At Home agency but guessed it was half-an-hour ago. He would get something to eat, then head back to the agency and hope Ms. Gomez-Martin would see him.

He stumbled upon an ice cream and sandwich shop and ordered a grilled cheese.

"Chips with it?" the waitperson asked.

"How about coleslaw?"

"Sorry."

"Chips then. And coffee, black."

Ms. Gomez-Martin was in her office when he got back to the agency. She was a woman in her fifties with hair going gray in a becoming way. She spoke with a barely perceptible accent, the faint remnant of the native tongue she had long ago left behind.

"I will try to be helpful, Judge Randall, but I cannot reveal medical details of our clients."

"I understand completely."

"Roberta told me why you're here, and I can tell you that Mr. Mitchell was under our care for seven months before he died. We rotated several nurses through his home before we found a pair who could put up with him."

"He was a difficult patient?"

"If there were combat pay for home care nurses, Maria and Jennifer would have deserved it. How they put up with him, I don't know. They had the ability to make him relent by turning his growls back at him, with a bit of faux-flattery attached. I guess that is how they survived."

"Where are they now?"

"Jennifer has returned to her native Philippines, and we assigned Maria to an elderly couple in the Pioneer Valley."

"I would like to talk to them. Mitchell may have inadvertently said something that could help solve a crime. They may not even realize the import of what he said. Will you ask them if they'll talk to me, please?"

"They may refuse, but okay. Give me a few days and I'll see what I can do."

*

Jim and Pat were eating dinner in his kitchen when the doorbell rang. Jim's townhouse was long front-to-back and it took him an age to get to the front door. Which had its advantages because he loathed solicitors interrupting his dinner. When they waited him out and were still there when he opened the door, he would beat them to the pitch, saying, don't take this personally but I never give to people who interrupt my dinner, goodbye.

"Who was it?" Pat asked, when Jim got back to the table. They were eating leftover Whole Foods meatloaf, which was stale when purchased and now tasted like sawdust.

"Another Worthy Cause, Inc."

"Oh, what a grouch you are. Do you have any hope?"

"That door-to-door solicitors will leave me alone?"

"No, I meant getting one or both of Mitchell's nurses to talk to you."

Jim lowered his fork. "I don't know. If neither nurse will talk to me, I don't know what I'll do."

Out the kitchen window, the light was gathering for a dramatic departure. Darker by the minute, a thin band of light coating the horizon.

"Do you see the light, Jim?"

"I do."

"Metaphor, Jim. Metaphor."

The phone rang. Jim grumbled, "First the doorbell, now the phone."

"Well, are you going to answer?"

He grumbled but answered. "Hello?"

"Judge Randall, this is Ms. Gomez-Martin of the Safe At Home agency. I'm sorry to be calling at dinnertime, but I reached both nurses and I thought you'd want to know what they said as soon as I heard."

"You are correct."

"I'm sorry, Judge, neither is willing to speak to you."

"Did either give a reason?"

"Maria in the Pioneer Valley says she has put her time with Mr. Mitchell behind her and has no wish to re-live it. And Jennifer in the Philippines fears not being allowed back into the United States. There are visa issues, Judge Randall. Try to understand."

"I do, but I'm very disappointed. Would it help if I wrote them a personal letter?"

"Can't hurt."

"Would you get the letters to them?"

"I see no harm in that."

Pat saw the disappointment in Jim's face when he got off the phone. "What a shame," she said.

Jim grimaced. "I need to put a lot of thought into these letters, not dash them off. Why should the nurses help a stranger? How can I persuade them?"

"You'll find a way. You can be very persuasive when you curb your impatience."

*

Dear Maria,

My name is Jim Randall. I was a judge on the Massachusetts Superior Court for twenty-one years. Since my retirement, I have become something of an amateur detective, helping the authorities solve crimes that interest me.

Before his death, you took care of a man named Stan Mitchell. He and I were law school classmates, and I was in the audience when he died, which was a shock to everyone there. My interest in the circumstances surrounding his death was aroused when a man he had been feuding with – Arthur Maplewood – died a few days later. Coincidences like that intrigue and challenge me. Coincidences are a fact of life but extreme coincidences make me suspicious.

I would very much like to talk to you. Can you spare me a few minutes? I am interested in anything that Mr. Mitchell might have said or done in his final months that may, in hindsight, shed light on his death. Did he suspect that someone wished him harm? Did he express any unusual fears? Did he utter any threats? Those are the kind of questions I want to ask, and nothing I ask could get you in trouble. I am not interested in second-guessing the nursing care you provided, I am interested in Stan's state of mind before he died.

I have come to understand – from my conversations with people who knew him – that Stan over the years had become a disagreeable guy. You may want nothing more to do with him. Or you may feel he was unfairly maligned. Either way, talking to me could help set the record straight. Any man or woman, no matter how mean, deserves to be treated with dignity when they die. Please help me. I await your reply.

10

He wrote the letter in his study, using a pen to make it as personal as possible. He had not handwritten a letter for years, and his fingers felt their age when he finished. As he stood from his desk, his legs felt stiffer than usual: to advance in age is to approach the condition of wood.

He creaked his way down two flights of stairs; by the time he had reached the second floor, his legs felt looser, and by the time he reached the first floor, where Pat was writing at the kitchen table, his legs felt like rubber.

He handed Pat the letter. "Will you read this for me? Same letter will go to both nurses."

Pat was working on her laptop at the kitchen table. She took the letter, read it and handed it back.

"Well?" he asked, when she didn't say anything.

"I think it's good. I'm a little surprised at your personal tone. Your writing is usually stiff."

"My writing is usually stiff?"

"Formal. Your judicial writings were concise and clear, that's what made them so good, but they were formal. Relax, I'm on your side."

He lowered his eyes, a schoolboy being scolded by a teacher. "Are you suggesting I'm overly touchy?"

"A little."

"But I accept praise easily, don't I?"

"Oh, very easily."

"So it evens out, does it not. Duck, Duck, Goose for dinner?"

*

He checked in with Ms. Gomez-Martin often during the next few weeks. Had either of the nurses responded to his letter?

"Jennifer in the Philippines is afraid she will never be allowed back into the United States if she talks to you."

"How about the nurse in the Pioneer Valley?"

"Maria? No, I have heard nothing from her. I'll let you know if I do."

Jim wasn't ready to admit defeat. Who could he talk to who knew what it was like to follow leads that lead nowhere? Sasha Cohen.

He invited Sasha to join him at The Long Gone the next morning.

She pulled her chair closer to the table. "How are you doing, Jim?"

"I'm depressed. I usually just get grumpy."

"This sounds serious."

"I don't want to overdo the pathos, but I'm at a dead end. What do you do when your sources don't pan out?"

Sasha's face softened. "Who have you spoken to?"

"The relatives and business associates of Stan Mitchell and Arthur Maplewood that I've been able to find. Mitchell had 24 hour nursing care. I tried to reach his nurses but struck out. Any suggestions?"

"When I am pursuing a story, I construct a scenario in my head to give me a framework to hang my facts on. Have you done that?"

"Yes. I tried the scenario that Maplewood murdered Mitchell to stop him from acquiring Maplewood Naturals.

Now I lean towards Mitchell killing Maplewood to get him out of the way and allow the takeover to happen. If that is what happened, it leaves open the question of why Mitchell died the same week."

"Do you have any guesses?"

Jim shrugged his shoulders. "Stan Mitchell was a very sick man and knew he didn't have long to live. Maybe he saw the opportunity to get away with murder. Who would suspect a dead man?"

The Long Gone had fallen completely silent while he spoke, at least it seemed so to Jim. Sasha started to reply, but Jim held up his hand. "Hold on a second, maybe I've stumbled on the perfect crime. Mitchell murdered Maplewood knowing that he, Mitchell, was about to die, which meant he'd be an unlikely suspect. Maybe he killed himself on stage to be sure he had witnesses that he died while Maplewood was still alive."

"Suicide?"

"Giving death a helping hand. He was a very sick man."

"Ingenious, if true, but how do you prove it?" Sasha said.

"At the moment, I can't. Mitchell had round the clock nursing care, but the nurses who cared for Mitchell in his final days won't talk to me."

Sasha let her eyes drift around the coffee shop while she wrote the story in her mind. "I hope your scenario is right. It would make a terrific story."

"At the moment, it's fiction, so you can't use it."

"But wouldn't it be delicious?" Sasha exclaimed.

"Not the word I would use. Sordid, depraved, I'd say. Which man, Mitchell or Maplewood, was the most likely to be that depraved, do you think?"

"My reporting says that both men had tempers and egos, but everything I've learned so far says that Stan Mitchell despised anything and everything no matter how small, how trivial, that stood in his way. Maplewood, on the other hand, only became a beast when something he loved – something he had built – was about to be taken from him. Jim, I have to get back to my office."

"I'm in my office," Jim replied.

"You've made me into a Long Gone fan. Which way are you heading?"

"Home, I guess."

They left The Long Gone and walked towards Harvard Square. As they walked, Jim said. "I need to learn more about the private Stan Mitchell. Maybe Isabel, Mitchell's second wife, will meet with me again. She was open with me before."

They passed Cambridge Hospital.

"My late wife, Joyce, died in this hospital. I don't actively miss her the way I used to, but the hospital brings it all back to me. It's so hard to shake the image of someone on their death bed."

"I can't imagine."

"I'm lucky to have Pat. We rarely fight, we squabble but rarely fight. It helps to have neutral corners to retreat to."

"She intimidates me."

"She intimidates a lot of people. If you think she's intimidating now, you should have seen her on the bench." Pause. "A lot of people think I'm intimidating."

"You? You're a pussycat."

"Here's my street. The quickest way to the T is to cut through the high school."

"You think I don't know my beat, Jim? Do you think I don't know my way? I'm a seasoned reporter. Lean down."

He did as he was told, and she kissed him on the cheek.

"Do you do that to all your sources?" he asked.

"You bet. How do you think I get my scoops?" And she waved goodbye as she crossed the street.

His house was dark as usual when he entered. His front room got little light in the middle of the day. His study got superb light in the early morning but the best of it had faded by the time Jim climbed the stairs, sat down at his desk, and reached for his fountain pen.

Dear Maria,

I understand why you might not want to talk, but let me bring you up-to-date. I am presently operating on the theory that Stan Mitchell may have had something to do with the death of Arthur Maplewood and you may have overheard him say something that could shed light on the matter. Maybe something that didn't seem significant at the time.

He put down his pen and waggled his fingers to keep them from getting stiff.

Let me tell you a little more about myself. I was a judge for twenty-one years. I retired at age 65 and stumbled into what I am doing now, helping the district attorney and the

*police solve crimes. There are times when people speak more
freely to a retired judge than they do to a DA or the police.
Besides, judging cases for twenty-one years gave me a unique
vantage point from which to view crime. The police, of
necessity, face crime head-on; I had the luxury of viewing
it from a judge's bench. It looks different from that angle,
believe me.*

*If you ever want to talk, I can drive out to where you are
very easily. The Pioneer Valley is one of my favorite parts
of Massachusetts, a state where I've lived my whole working
life (I also have a house in Vermont that my late wife and I
bought years ago). If after we talk, it is clear you heard or
saw nothing of relevance while caring for Stan Mitchell, so
be it. No matter what, I pledge you will not get in trouble
because of anything you might tell me. You have my word.*

*I'll repeat my contact information in case you change
your mind and want to talk. I'm guessing there are things
about Stan Mitchell's death that don't add up, and that
talking with me might help settle your mind once and for all.
No matter what you decide to do, I wish you well.*

He crossed the room to his chair and lowered himself
into it. Cicero beckoned but Jim lacked the energy to lift
himself out of his chair and pluck a volume off the shelves.

*

Isabel, Stan Mitchell's second wife, agreed to meet with
Jim again. They met as before at the Route 2 pizza place
with the empty parking lot.

She was there when he arrived.

"You got here before me last time too," he said, sitting down across from her.

"I don't like to be late."

"Thanks for meeting with me again."

"No problem. Are you making progress?"

"No. And I'm not happy about it. I keep going back and forth between possible scenarios. What was Stan like at home when you and he were married?"

"How long do you have? Stan was not an easy man to live with or explain."

"So I gather. What, specifically?"

"Since we talked I've thought a lot about Stan's avariciousness, his insatiable ego, his incredibly thin skin, his need to always be first and best. No one else existed in his world of one, although he was good at charming people when he needed them. Switching from litigation to deal making was about getting rich, to be sure, but more about ego, and his entire ego was at stake with every deal. When he realized Arthur might win his fight to maintain control of Maplewood Naturals and, on top of that, had filed an ethics complaint against Stan, I can see Arthur becoming a mortal menace in Stan's eyes."

"Interesting. Do you think Stan dying on the dais while he was being honored was a coincidence or did he take a hand in the timing?"

"Suicide?"

"Hastening a disease process that was going to kill him anyway."

"Why would he do that?"

"To eliminate himself as a suspect in the death of Arthur Maplewood."

"What are you suggesting, that Stan killed Arthur?"

"I'm considering all possibilities. There was bad blood between the two and a business reason to get Arthur out of the way, and Stan sounds ruthless enough to do it. "

"I ended up despising Stan, but murder? That's too big a stretch, but I can see him taking a hand in his own demise. Stan liked to make as big a splash as possible, and what bigger splash could there be than dying when you're the guest of honor at your law school reunion."

"Wouldn't he have left a note to brag about what he had done?"

"Not necessarily. Stan took enormous pride in outfoxing everyone. He might have wanted to be the only person who knew what he had done. You were in the audience when he died – did he have a smug smile on his face?"

"Not that I noticed, but I take your point. So, no note. How long were Stan and his third wife married?"

"Less than a year. They barely had time to get to know each other. He married her on the rebound after I divorced him. She had been a model when she was young and looked good on his arm. Their marriage ended maybe fifteen years ago, and I heard she quickly remarried and moved to Arizona. Stan must have decided that three tries was enough because he never married again."

"And the first wife?"

"I have no idea what happened to her after she and Stan divorced. That was long ago, they were kids."

"Is there anybody else you can think of who might know something pertinent about him?"

"At work, Stan only trusted Glen Hudson. He had a very small staff and Glen Hudson was his number two. It's inconceivable to me that Stan confided in anyone except Glen. He believed the knives would come out at the first sign of weakness."

"He had no children of his own, correct?"

"Correct, which is fortunate. I wouldn't wish Stan as a father on any child."

"You didn't want children?"

"I did but couldn't. Which was a relief to him. He didn't want the competition for my attention."

"He sounds absolutely dreadful. I'm surprised *you* didn't kill him."

"Believe me, the thought crossed my mind. But as dreadful as he was, he never laid a hand on me. There was that to be said in his favor."

"Faint praise."

"How about you, Judge Randall. Are you married?"

"I was for thirty years to Joyce, who died a dozen years ago. Now I am involved with a former colleague on the court. Why did a hint of amusement cross your face as I said that?"

"She must be quite a woman to handle you."

"How should I take that?"

"As flattery. You're a formidable man."

"Now you've embarrassed me."

She smiled. "Good."

When they parted in the near empty parking lot, it crossed Jim's mind that she may have been coming on to him. It had been so long since anyone had that he had forgotten the signals.

He drove out of the parking lot and headed east on Route 2.

"Nah, you're imagining things," he told himself at the stoplight. But recently he had been feeling so old and defeated it was nice to feel desirable again, even if it was all in his imagination.

11

Two nights later, Jim and Pat went to Duck, Duck, Goose for dinner. Bruce at the front desk was as nice as usual, the restaurant looked as good as usual, but Jim didn't like the night's menu, and he groused about it to Pat.

"Are they abandoning what has made them so good? Is nothing sacred?"

"What's wrong, Jim? Why are you in such a bad mood?"

He put down the menu and leaned back in his chair. "I don't know. Yes, I do. I've lost heart. I should never have taken this case. In the future, I'll make sure there is a crime before I jump in." He picked up the menu and ran his eyes down the list. "I don't know what the hell redfish is."

"A fish sort of like cod."

"Why doesn't it say cod?"

"Because it's redfish."

He glared over the menu at Pat. "It's a good thing we didn't move in together."

"You said it."

"I need a fanciful woman."

"No doubt."

"You're too reality based."

"God forbid."

He lowered the menu again. "I feel much better. Thank you."

"Anytime. What are you going to eat?"

"Redfish. It's one of my favorites."

Jim took Pat's hand on the short walk to his townhouse.

"Are you being affectionate because you feel defeated?" Pat asked.

"No, ma'am. I'm being affectionate to keep you from thinking you've figured me out."

She leaned against his arm under a streetlamp. "You are so unpredictable, you're predictable. That's what I love about you."

"Keep 'em guessing. Never get pinned down."

A voicemail was waiting when they reached his townhouse. Jim listened to it in the kitchen.

The woman had a slight accent. "Judge Randall, this is Maria Hernandez. I'm responding to your letters. If you wish to talk, please call me."

Jim jotted down her number. "You'll never guess who that was."

"Tell me."

"One of Stan Mitchell's former nurses, the one who now works in the Pioneer Valley. I'm stunned to hear from her."

He called the number she had left.

Her voice sounded tentative when she answered. "Yes?"

"This is Judge Randall. Is this Maria Hernandez?"

"Yes. Hello, Judge. I should tell you, I am very nervous about talking to you. I am here on a work visa that expires soon and I don't want to be sent home."

"Where is home?"

"Guatemala."

"Your immigration status won't be affected by our conversation. I am investigating a possible murder and that is my only reason for talking to you. I'd rather do this in person. Can we meet somewhere?"

"I'm taking care of an elderly couple in Amherst. I can't travel to Boston."

"I'll come to you. I would like to bring my partner, Pat Knowles. She was a judge on the same court as I."

"Why do you want to bring her?"

"Two heads are better than one. You can trust her totally. But if you'd rather I come alone, that's fine with me."

She paused briefly. "No, she can come. There is a coffee shop in North Amherst, close to where I work. Can we meet there?" She gave Jim the name and address.

She only had every other Monday off, so there was a wait of almost two weeks before Jim and Pat could drive to Amherst and meet with her. Jim used the time to ready his questions:

Did Stan Mitchell talk about his life while you were caring for him? Did he talk about his victories, his regrets? Did he become more talkative as the end neared? Did he indicate when he expected the end to be? Did he express anger at anybody? Did he talk at all about business? Did he ever mention the name Arthur Maplewood?

Pat and Jim drove out on the first day of actual spring as opposed to calendar spring. Route 2 is not a bucolic road, but it traverses pleasant countryside, and the warmth of the sun felt good in Jim's car.

"How open do you think she'll be?" Pat asked after they were past the traffic circle near Concord. A state prison was located on the circle, barbed wire and all, such a contrast to an old Yankee town like Concord.

"Don't know. Over the phone she sounded hesitant. On the other hand, she did call me. I suspect how open she'll be will depend on how comfortable she is with us."

Route 2 winds through and over hills. On certain tight curves the speed limit drops from 55 to 45, but no one ever slows down, so drivers who obey the law are risking their lives. Jim drove with all deliberate speed, not to be intimidated by impatient truckers. By the time he reached the turnoff for Route 202, he was relieved to be off the main road.

"Do you know where we're going?" Pat asked.

"Approximately."

"You really ought to learn to use GPS."

"And turn my driving over to an algorithm? Not a chance."

He pulled to a stop and backed up. Looking out the rear window for the turn he had missed, he growled, "Don't you dare. Not a word."

The coffee shop was on a bend in the road surrounded by what looked like forest. When they entered the shop, Jim was struck by its hybrid nature: not a pure-bred coffee shop like The Long Gone. A deli/coffee/sandwich shop. He liked the atmosphere; funky, trendy, intellectual.

He spotted a petite dark-haired woman sitting in a corner. A window over her left shoulder cast a glare that obscured her face but he knew it was Maria when she waved. It was the tentative wave of someone asking, "Are you the right people?"

Jim glanced at Pat, who nodded; she had seen Maria, too.

They headed to Maria's table. The shop was busy but, being a Monday, not packed. A handful of people waited at the counter to order. Jim and Pat brushed by them and approached. Jim recognized Maria from his law school reunion; she had been the nurse who wheeled Stan Mitchell onstage and hovered in the wings while he was honored.

"Maria?"

"Yes. Sit down, please."

They did. "I'm Jim Randall, and this is Pat Knowles, my former colleague on the court and current companion."

"Pleased to meet you." In person, Maria Hernandez had a pleasant face and gentle manner. When she spoke, Jim sensed someone who had been pushed around by life, but who managed to retain a friendly nature.

"We have a lot to talk about," Jim said. "Are you in a rush?"

"No, this is my day off."

"Then I'm going to get myself some coffee. Pat?"

"Tea, please."

"May I get you a refill?" he asked Maria.

"No, I'm fine."

Jim went to the counter. The line moved swiftly and in a few minutes he came back with a coffee and a tea.

He sat down and said, "Thanks for agreeing to meet with us. I have a house in Vermont not too far north of here. I love this part of the country. Do you like it?"

She nodded, diffident, watchful. "I do, but I miss the city. I grew up in Guatemala City."

"How long did you work for Stan Mitchell?"

"Seven months. I lasted longer than any other nurse. Mr. Mitchell was a difficult man."

"Tell us about that. How was he difficult?"

The ambient noise in the shop faded into the background, and all Jim heard was Maria's sturdy, soothing voice. "Nothing was good enough for Mr. Mitchell. The bed wasn't made right, the food not hot enough, the windows were open too wide or not wide enough. Mr. Mitchell believed – he truly believed – that people were always out to get him. That included me at first."

"Yet you didn't quit."

"I understood him, I didn't take what he said personally. He felt let down by everyone. You would not believe the terrible things he said about his ex-wives. The only one he said anything nice about was his second wife, Isabel, but she left him and he could never forgive her for that. When he said bad things about my work, I would laugh with my eyes and say, 'Yes, yes, Mr. Mitchell, anything you say, Mr. Mitchell.' He did not like that at first but he didn't fire me, and eventually he chuckled when I did that. I think he liked people who weren't afraid of him."

"Except people like Arthur Maplewood."

Maria shook her head. "He could not *stand* Arthur Maplewood! Could not stand him! I wanted to wash my ears out with soap whenever he talked about Arthur Maplewood."

"Do you remember anything specific he said about him?"

"Let me think. Sore loser, that was one thing he said. Dishonest whiner. A weak man, a very weak man. Not willing to accept reality. Those were the kind of things he said."

"Sounds like he was describing himself."

She nodded. "He did that all the time."

"Was he angry at anyone else?"

"Isabel, for leaving him."

"Anybody from his business life?"

"Not that I overheard. Only Arthur Maplewood."

Pat had been listening intently. Now she asked, "Did Mr. Mitchell realize how ill he was?"

"Not all the time. Sometimes he talked as if he'd get better in a few days."

"Do you think he knew when the end was finally approaching?"

Maria thought about that. "Yes, I think he did. He became more subdued near the end. He talked about his childhood, how lonely he had been, how strong it had made him. Then, on the day of his reunion, he grew agitated. I could barely keep him in his wheelchair."

"Could that have been excitement at the prospect of being honored in front of his classmates?"

"It could be, but I sensed deep sadness, and when he died, I felt guilty because I had not understood."

"Did you change his medications near the end?"

"No. I gave him the same meds every day."

Pat said, "Yet the postmortem showed a lower level of blood pressure medication than prescribed."

"I can't explain that. I counted out his meds every week, and checked to make sure he had taken them. Maybe he deceived me."

Jim said, "The medical examiner determined the cause of death was cardiac arrest caused by the failure of his pacemaker. Had Mr. Mitchell complained of an irregular heartbeat before he died?"

"No. In the months I worked with him, he only reported one incident where his heartbeat sped out of control. He said his pacemaker kicked in and he felt a stronger jolt than expected. He said it felt like a mule kicking him in the chest. He was paranoid about the pacemaker. He had me check the placement of the electrodes regularly."

"Wait a minute, you checked the placement of the electrodes? Are you saying his pacemaker was external?"

"Yes. He needed a pacemaker but was too weak to tolerate the procedure, so his doctors prescribed an external pacemaker until he was strong enough to have a pacemaker implanted in his chest."

Jim looked at Pat. She nodded.

"Think hard about this. Did he ever express a wish to end it all?"

"Suicide? Is that what you mean?"

"Yes."

"Never. Stan Mitchell was more likely to kill Arthur Maplewood than himself."

"Did you ever hear him threaten to kill Maplewood?"

"No. I just knew he hated him."

"Final question. Did he have visitors in the days immediately before he died?"

"Yes, his doctor, and a business associate, I don't remember his name."

"Glen Hudson?"

"That's him."

Jim and Pat didn't stay much longer. "You have been very helpful. We're grateful. If we have more questions, may we call you?"

"Yes. Everybody hated Mr. Mitchell, and I did too on some days. But he knew I understood him, so eventually he was nice to me." She stopped. "You promised that I won't get in trouble for talking to you."

"And I meant it."

Jim and Pat drove straight back to Boston. On the way, Jim asked, "So what do you think?"

"A woman incapable of telling a lie. A woman who knew what kind of man Stan Mitchell was, but found things to like about him. He was lucky she was his nurse near the end."

Jim murmured, "I agree." The roller coaster road lifted them up and dropped them back down. It was getting late in the afternoon.

A sign read: rest stop half a mile ahead. "I'm going to try to reach Glen Hudson before he leaves his office."

Jim pulled into the rest stop. Hudson had gone for the day.

"I'll give you his voicemail, Judge Randall."

Jim left a message requesting another meeting to, as Jim put it, "iron out a few inconsistencies in the stories I'm hearing about you, before I go to the press."

It worked. Jim was summoned to Hudson's State Street office two days later. Hudson looked no happier to see him than the first time; if anything his expression had hardened.

"Inconsistencies?" he said before Jim was seated.

"Did you or Mitchell make the decision to acquire Maplewood Naturals?"

Hudson's eyes narrowed further. "Stan. Why?"

"Apparently he was in terrible physical shape, and I'm wondering how he could have mustered the energy and will to pursue the takeover of a thriving company, an unusual takeover attempt for him in the best of times."

"You didn't know Stan. A weak body but a very determined man."

"I knew him in law school. What did you think of his decision?"

"I was against it at first, as I told you, but I changed my mind. I think the takeover attempt gave Stan something to live for and kept him alive longer than otherwise."

"You told me when we met that he wanted to control a thriving company to balance the risks of acquiring bankrupt companies. Was there any other reason?"

"You already know the answer to that, am I right?"

"I know he hated Arthur Maplewood, and I understand the business reasons for hating him, but were there hidden reasons he might have confided to you but not to others?"

"When Stan took a dislike to someone, he became possessed and Arthur Maplewood had the type of too-good-to-be-true persona and sterling reputation that Stan couldn't abide."

"So there was a knock-the-good-guy-off-his-perch aspect to it?"

"For sure. Stan didn't believe anybody was good at heart, only for show."

"Yet you stayed with Mitchell Equity for years. How did you manage?"

"I have a little bit of Stan in me. We got along."

"But eventually he got too weak to be personally involved in day-to-day business, is that right?"

"Near the very end, yes."

"At that point did you take the lead in the takeover attempt of Maplewood Naturals?"

"Yes, I represented our firm at the final meetings with Arthur Maplewood and his people, but I coordinated everything with Stan. Why are you so interested in the minutiae of the deal?"

"I couldn't care less about the deal. My concern is the double deaths."

"And you think I had something to do with one or both." Hudson stated that matter-of-factly, not as a question.

"Did you?"

Hudson cackled. "Yeah, killed 'em both!" Hudson laughed so hard he had trouble breathing. Abruptly, he swivelled his chair away from Jim. "Any more questions?"

Jim rose. "No. You've told me what I need to know. Thank you for your time."

Jim walked out into the sunshine. He had gone into the meeting with only the vaguest idea of what he hoped to accomplish, and now wondered if he had accomplished anything. Had Hudson just admitted guilt? Or by his "confession" was he mocking Jim? The latter, most likely. Make a fool of yourself, why don't you, Jim?

Jim's internal GPS had a default setting of Ted Conover's office. His feet headed there now. He called as he walked.

"Ted, I'm at an inflection point. Can you spare me five minutes?"

"Get here in five, and I'll spare you two."

"Deal."

Ted looked at his watch when Jim arrived out of breath. "Ten minutes. I'll give you one. Sit down."

"I just met with Stan Hudson, Stan Mitchell's trusted number two. He represented Mitchell at the final meetings with Arthur Maplewood. Can you do a quick background check on Hudson for me?"

Jim was still breathing hard.

"Don't keel over in my office please," Ted said. "I've done a lot of favors for you, cut a lot of corners, but I draw the line at giving you CPR."

"What kind of public servant are you?"

"A busy one. Yes, I'll run Hudson through our computers. Now I am late for a meeting about an actual crime, if you catch my drift."

Jim headed towards The Long Gone when he left Ted's office. Before he got there he took out his phone and called Maria Hernandez in Amherst.

"Did I catch you at a bad time?" Jim asked.

"No. My patients are both taking a nap."

"Did you overhear anything Glen Hudson said to Stan Mitchell during his final visits?"

"They mostly talked business."

"Can you remember anything specific?"

"I was going in and out of the room, so I wasn't paying close attention, but I do remember Mr. Hudson saying he thought the stockholders of Mr. Maplewood's company would vote in favor of the acquisition if Arthur Maplewood wasn't standing in the way."

"Do you remember Mr. Mitchell's reaction?"

"He said something like, that's what I think too. And then he asked me to leave the room."

12

Jim started to mentally construct his case at The Long Gone, continued it on the walk home past his touchstones – Beauty Shop Row and the live poultry store – and was still constructing it when Pat arrived at his townhouse to spend the night.

They ate a late dinner in Jim's kitchen.

"Glen Hudson is too smug for his own good. Too smug and maybe more deadly. Here's what I think as of," Jim glanced at the wall clock, "7:18 p.m. Stan Mitchell enlisted Hudson to poison Arthur Maplewood, and once that was in motion, hastened his own death by disabling his pacemaker, thereby removing himself as a suspect in Maplewood's death."

"Jim, you love to crawl out on limbs, the longer the better."

"Why is that far-fetched?"

"Glen Hudson sounds to me like a manipulator, a facilitator, but not a contract killer. Why would he do Mitchell's dirty work for him, dirty work in this case being murder? Sounds far-fetched to me."

"What if Hudson stood to benefit from Arthur Maplewood's death? What if there was financial gain in it for him?"

"Jim, I love you, and admire you, but now you've gone too far."

A long silence followed. Jim toyed with his desert. Blueberry crisp he had bought at a nearby convenience store. He poked it with his fork as if he were trying to get it to move.

Finally he sat up straight, eyebrows arched, eyes distant. "Nailed it."

"Nailed what?"

"Behold, the genius amateur detective! Sleuthing at its best."

"Jim, whatever are you talking about?"

He rose from the table.

"The missing piece of the puzzle." His plan wouldn't be easy, it wasn't foolproof. It involved a little bit of deception, a little bit of manipulation, not his usual working method, but with both principals dead, unusual methods were called for. "I'm going up to my study. I'll do the cleanup later."

Jim climbed the stairs, his legs feeling spongy. Would he be able to make it to the top? You are being overly dramatic, he told himself. Just because you discovered a path forward doesn't mean you've solved the case. Be a little less manic.

He made it to his desk without a hitch and called Ted while looking out his window at a black-on-black sky. "Sorry to call you so late, Ted. But you won't deny that my friendship makes up for my frequent interruptions."

"I will neither confirm nor deny. In case you're calling to learn what I've found so far about Glen Hudson, his name cropped up during an SEC investigation of securities fraud a dozen years ago. The case was dropped and Hudson was never the target of the investigation but his name was mentioned by more than one witness. That's all a quick computer search revealed." Ted paused. "Is that what you wanted to know?"

"Yes, but that's not why I'm calling. I'm calling to ask your permission to mention your name."

"To whom?"

"Maria Hernandez, Mitchell's nurse in his final days. She'll be afraid to do what I ask, but if she knows her cooperation won't hurt her visa status, she might. Her work visa will expire soon, and she doesn't want to go back to Guatemala."

"You'll have to do better than that."

"Would you put in a word for her with immigration if she agreed to help me catch a killer?"

"Too cryptic by half, Jim. What are you saying?"

"If I can persuade Maria to join me in a meeting with Glen Hudson, I think we can get him to make a mistake."

"I think I see where you're going with this, but spell it out."

"I couldn't figure out why Hudson would agree to kill Arthur Maplewood, but then the obvious hit me: Mitchell had promised Hudson that he could take over Maplewood Naturals once it was in Mitchell's portfolio and Arthur Maplewood was out of the way."

"Jim, we've known each other a long time, and normally I trust your judgement, but do you realistically believe Glen Hudson will agree to meet with you and the nurse who cared for Mitchell in his final days? If you're right and Hudson was Mitchell's poison-bearer, won't Hudson tell you in anatomically precise detail how and where to fuck yourself?"

"Maybe, but maybe not. He's a finance guy who's about to get very rich, and guys like that often have an inflated opinion of their abilities, think they can get away with anything."

"Including murder?"

"Yes, including murder, if the incentive is big enough."

Ted didn't respond.

"Ted?" Jim finally inquired.

"I think this time the limb you've crawled out on will break and you will fall, but okay to use my name to persuade Maria Hernandez to help you."

"Thanks, Ted. I owe you one."

"One? How' bout a thousand? Oh, heck, how about a million?"

Jim rose from his desk and went down to the kitchen.

"You look smug," Pat said when she saw him. "What did you do up there?"

Jim joined her at the table. "Solve a murder."

He waited until the next day before he put his plan into motion. First step, call Maria Hernandez.

"Good morning, this is Judge Randall. Do you have a moment for me to bring you up-to-date?"

"This is not a good time. Can I call you this afternoon?"

"Yes, that's fine."

She didn't call back until 3. "I can talk now, my clients are napping. They are sweet people and it scares me to think what will happen when one of them dies. They keep each other alive. Why did you call?"

"I have a plan to catch Arthur Maplewood's killer, but I need your help. As you know because you were there, Glen Hudson met with Arthur Maplewood several times to discuss the acquisition of Maplewood Naturals.

During those meetings I believe he gradually poisoned Maplewood."

Maria didn't answer.

"Are you there?" Jim asked after a minute.

"Yes." Maria sounded meek.

"Will you help me?"

Another long pause. "What do you want from me?"

Jim explained what he had in mind. As he heard his plan spoken aloud, he grew increasingly skeptical about it, and if he felt that way about his own plan, how would she feel?

"It sounds dangerous," she said when he had finished. "If Mr. Hudson would poison Mr. Maplewood, why won't he kill me?"

"We'll do it in a public place, and I'll be with you."

"I don't know. My visa."

"Helping catch a criminal will be of great help in extending your visa. Take your time. No need to decide now."

Jim had taken the call in the living room, which meant Pat overheard. When he got off the phone, he asked Pat, "Am I putting her in danger?"

"Possibly. Why do you need her? Can't you just tell Hudson that she is willing to testify as to what she overheard?"

"Hudson won't believe me. He'll think I'm trying to trick him. He needs to hear it from her."

"You have no right to jeopardize Maria's safety."

Jim didn't take kindly to that. "You think I don't know that? You think I'm cavalier about putting people in danger?"

"Calm down, Jim. I know you would never willingly put people in danger, but you have a tendency to get carried away. All I'm saying is, be careful."

*

Even if Maria agreed to a meeting, Jim needed Glen Hudson's buy-in too. Hudson agreed to give Jim five minutes in his State Street office the following day. On the phone he did not sound smug, he sounded afraid. Why? Did he sense things closing in? Was that why he agreed to meet with Jim again?

Hudson sat stoically behind his desk. His hair still resembled newly poured asphalt but his face now looked like the rocky roadbed before asphalt is poured. "You don't give up, do you?" he began.

"Not when I'm close to solving a crime."

"Oh?"

"You were overheard telling Stan Mitchell that you thought the Maplewood Naturals stockholders would vote for the acquisition if Arthur Maplewood stopped blocking it."

Steel. Hudson's expression didn't change. "So?"

"Subsequently you met with Maplewood on several occasions to persuade him to vote for the acquisition. When he refused, you and Mitchell decided to take matters into your own hands."

Hudson shook his head as if to say, "Is that the best you can do?"

"And the nurse who overheard your conversation with Mitchell is ready to tell her story to the DA."

Over Hudson's shoulder, a plane taking off from Logan diagonally crossed the window. By the time the plane was gone, Hudson's expression had changed from steel to ice. Both cold, one subject to melting. His left eyebrow quivered. "I don't believe you."

"Suit yourself. I won't shed a tear if you go to jail."

"You're full of shit." Hudson stood. "I don't get it. What's in this for you?"

"Once a judge, always a judge. Besides, Stan and I were classmates in law school. My curiosity is both personal and professional. Give me the okay and I'll set up a meeting with you, me, and the nurse so you can hear for yourself."

"Not on your life."

"How about on yours?"

And then Maria got cold feet.

"Maria? Judge Randall calling. I talked to Glen Hudson about a meeting. He said no, but he's scared and I think he will come around."

Maria sounded embarrassed, defensive. "I"m sorry, Judge Randall, I changed my mind. Wait, my patient is calling me. Can you hold on?"

"Yes, I'll hold." Jim lowered the phone to his lap. He was alone in his living room, which seemed especially empty all of a sudden. If Maria backed out, he was done for. His first failure as a detective: could his ego take it?

"Judge? Are you still there?"

Hastily grabbing the phone off his lap, "Yes, I'm here."

"Are you mad at me?"

"No, but you've changed your mind?"

"It's too big a chance. I don't want to go back to Guatemala. The visa people here, they don't listen to the whole picture. If they hear I am involved in a criminal investigation, they won't stop to think maybe I'm not the criminal, they'll just say, Visa Denied. I know them."

"The Assistant District Attorney will speak up for you. I'll speak up for you. We'll explain that you were helping to catch a suspected killer."

"I'm sorry, Judge Randall. You saw the law from a judge's bench, I see it as an immigrant. I am at the bottom looking up. It looks different from here."

"Will you let me come out there and try to change your mind?"

"No. I'm sorry."

Jim hung up feeling defeated, deflated, and eviscerated. He tested his legs before he stood, not sure they would hold him. But they did, so he walked stiffly to the kitchen and refilled his wine glass.

Standing at the counter, he spilled a little wine as he poured. He was not a man who habitually swore, but now he swore more inventively than he ever had, which didn't make him feel better, which led to a string of new invective, which in hindsight he wished he had jotted down for future use.

Still standing, he called Pat.

"Talk me off the cliff," he said.

"Which cliff?"

"The 'I hate to fail' cliff."

"Let me guess. Maria Hernandez?"

"Yes."

"I'm not surprised. She had little to gain and much to lose. Poor Jim. I feel badly for you."

"Don't patronize me."

"Okay, I don't feel badly for you."

"We both had plenty of cases overturned on appeal. Why does this feel worse?"

"On the bench we had our robes and our gavels, as a sleuth you're naked. Why don't you come here for the night?"

"The idea of walking to the T and climbing your damned hill are too much for me tonight."

"Try to get some sleep, Jim. You'll feel better in the morning."

13

Better being a relative term he did feel better in the morning, but not by much. And he remained subdued in spirit for days. He jogged his problem-solving imagination any way he could – by walking, by sitting by the Charles (moving water as problem solver), by lingering at The Long Gone – without results, except frustration.

Sasha Cohen's phone call changed that.

Jim was sitting at a middle table in The Long Gone when his phone did its little song and dance. He walked outside to take the call.

"It's Sasha, Jim."

"Hello, Sasha."

"Are you still investigating the deaths of Mitchell and Maplewood?"

"Yes, if sitting in The Long Gone waiting for inspiration to strike is considered investigating."

"The shareholders of Maplewood Naturals are being asked to vote on the acquisition next month. Did you know that?"

"No. I did not. When did this happen?"

"Our business reporter just got wind of it. An emergency meeting. Arthur Maplewood isn't cold in his grave and is about to lose his company. Somebody in the Mitchell camp anticipated his death for this to happen so soon."

"Glen Hudson."

"Excuse me?"

"Glen Hudson. Stan Mitchell's partner and accomplice in all things crooked."

"Do you have proof?"

"I have proof of nothing. I am sans-proof. I am proof-less."

"You sound bitter."

"Mitchell and Hudson must have planned this before Mitchell pulled the plug on his pacemaker," Jim said, as if he were talking to himself.

"Excuse me?"

"I think this was part of a master plan. Arthur Maplewood was standing in the way of Mitchell acquiring Maplewood Naturals, ergo Maplewood had to go. Mitchell got Glen Hudson to do the deed by promising to leave him a controlling interest in Maplewood Naturals after the takeover."

"But according to your story, Mitchell wouldn't be around to savor his victory."

"Correct. He only had a few days to live – a few weeks at most. I think the takeover had become an ego thing for Mitchell. Don't get in the way of Stan Mitchell, that's what it was about."

Sasha stayed silent for a minute. "This is prize winning stuff, Jim. I see a book, maybe a film. And don't forget, you owe me. Don't you dare give this to anyone else."

Jim chuckled. "You drive a hard bargain, Sasha."

"So how do we nail Glen Hudson?"

"For now, leave it to me. I have to make a few phone calls."

"Don't forget, you'll give me the exclusive. You promised."

Jim chuckled again. "I did not."

"Jim?"

"Okay, I promise, presupposing I'm right about this."

The phone calls Jim had in mind were to Vanessa and Donald Maplewood, but first a quick call to Ted.

Jim talked as he walked. "The Maplewood Naturals board doesn't waste time. They've called an emergency stockholder meeting next month to vote on whether or not to accept the buyout."

"Which suggests this was in the works before Mitchell and Maplewood died," Ted replied.

"Correct."

"Jim, I hope you're wrong. I'm getting tired of you stealing all my glory."

"You're handing me a straight line, but out of the goodness of my heart I shall let it pass. I'm almost home, I'll talk to you later."

He entered his darkened house and climbed straight to his light-filled study. Settling into his easy chair, surrounded by his books, he called Vanessa.

He was put straight through to her.

"I'm glad you called," she said. "I've been thinking about Dad at the end of his life, how elegiac and wary he seemed, which was unlike him. Remember what you said about Mitchell's second wife, Isabel?"

"That she thought Stan was slowly poisoning her."

"Yes. And I got to thinking how furious Stan Mitchell became when Dad filed his ethics complaint after refusing to sell his company, and I wonder if Dad feared for his life. Then I remembered a meeting I had with Mitchell's partner, Glen Hudson, while Mitchell was alive. Hudson wanted to know how involved I was with the day-to-day management of the company, and would I like to be more involved. He dangled the suggestion of a major role for me if he and Mitchell took control."

"What did you tell him?"

She gave a quiet laugh. "That he should go fuck his sorry self and pass the same message to his boss. I told him his questions were clumsy and offensive, that I was loyal to my dad, and that I would never vote my shares in favor of the acquisition."

"I've gotten to know Glen Hudson recently, and he is no match for you."

"He seemed chastened when he left my office, and I haven't heard from him since."

"Do you know if he approached your brother?"

"No, I don't, and I'm not sure Donald would tell me if he did. Donald is a strange man."

"I understand that the Maplewood board will vote on the acquisition at its next meeting."

"Yes. I was incensed when I learned about it. Dad's body isn't even cold."

"Were you and Donald consulted about the meeting?"

"I wasn't. I don't know about Donald."

Next, Jim called Donald.

He reached him on his farm. "Donald, it's Jim Randall," he said.

"Hi, Judge. I'm standing in a field that will be bursting with corn by the end of the summer. I always get excited when I think of soil's potential. What can I do for you?"

"I assume you know about the upcoming stockholders meeting?"

"Of course."

"You and your sister will own your father's shares once his will is probated. Between the two of you, you will control what happens to the company, isn't that right?"

"Yes. And your next question is, which way will I vote my shares?"

"Yes."

"I assume you have already talked to my beloved sister, who assumes I will sell out."

"Not in so many words."

"Well, she's right. I plan to vote my shares for Mitchell Equity to acquire Maplewood Naturals. What of it?"

"That's between you and your sister, and is none of my business. My business is murder. Specifically, your father's."

"That's your supposition. I don't believe Dad was murdered. He died from complications resulting from his long battle with diabetes."

"Officially, yes, but you might want to consider how your actions would look to a jury. A good lawyer can make it look as if you were in on a plot to murder your dad so you could inherit his shares and vote to sell his company to get very rich very fast."

"I loved Dad, and you can go to hell. I'm going to vote for the acquisition when I get my shares because Dad was stuck at the early stage of organics, the glory days when he had been Mr. Organics. Dad never did realize how the digital revolution had changed business. Maplewood Naturals will greatly grow its profits after Mitchell's firm acquires it, you wait and see."

The phone went dead. Jim stayed in his chair for a moment. The sky outside his window had become crosshatched with thin clouds while he talked, as if the cosmos sought to play tic-tac-toe. He lifted himself out of his chair and went downstairs, tightly gripping the banister all the way.

From the living room, he called Pat and asked if he could come over. Then he called Ted and was put through to his voice mail.

"Ted, it's Jim Randall. I'll explain later, but Donald Maplewood will vote to sell his father's company to Mitchell's firm. And the timing makes me think he had negotiated this with Mitchell's camp before his dad's death. To be continued."

As Jim walked across Harvard Yard on his way to the T and Pat's, he got Sasha Cohen on the phone.

"Donald Maplewood will vote in favor of the acquisition. Vanessa Maplewood will vote against it."

"So Donald is the bad guy?"

"Unclear. He certainly isn't loyal to his dad's memory, but there's no law against voting your shares as you see fit. On the other hand, there *is* a law against murder. Stan Mitchell and Glen Hudson conspired to slowly murder Arthur Maplewood, of that I'm now sure, but was Donald Maplewood their co-conspirator? Of that I'm not sure."

"Nice job," Sasha said. "How are you going to answer the question?"

"I have no idea. I wish you had stopped at 'nice job'."

The Red Line was packed. Breathing became territorial – hey, you're breathing my air, buddy, back off. He got off the subway at Charles Street and climbed Beacon Hill.

Pat tried to read his face when he reached her apartment. "You have your I-hate-the-human-race face on."

"You know the old saw about never reaching the goal line even though you get halfway to it with each play? That's the face I have on. Let's talk about it over dinner."

Duck, Duck, Goose taunted Jim that night: you thought familiar surroundings would relax you? Think again, pal. Jim had finished his first glass of wine (100% Cabernet Franc Chinon) when Pat reached across the table and took his hand. "Okay, tell me why you're especially frustrated today."

"Because I think I know whodunnit, but I don't know how to prove it."

The waiter came to take their order.

"Give me a second," Jim growled. "I haven't even looked at the menu."

"Take your time," the waiter said.

Jim looked across the table at Pat. "That makes me feel better."

"One growl and Jim cheers up."

"A bottle of wine, a single growl, and thou, my love." He touched Pat's glass and began to sing in a cracked monotone, "Young Donald had a farm, eei, eei, o, and on that farm he grew organics, want to go?"

Pat rolled her eyes. "Please. I beg you. Never ever, ever, do that again."

14

They drove to Vermont the next day, stopping at Jim's house for the night. They ate in the living room watching a veil of light hover over the Connecticut River valley. Jim was quiet during dinner. That in itself was not unusual, but the quality of tonight's quiet was different: a dense quiet, a thick quiet. When he and Pat were first getting to know each other as a couple, Pat was scared when Jim got this quiet, not knowing what it meant. She had learned the meaning of his silences – his puzzled quiet, his sardonic quiet, his bogged-down quiet – and was no longer afraid of them.

They left early in the morning for the long drive to Donald's farm on the western edge of Vermont.

Halfway across the state, Jim mused out loud. "I'm remembering the skillful cross-examinations I heard as a judge. The lawyers did not beat up on the witness, did not spring tricks on the witness. They got inside the witness' head, figured out where the switches and levers were, and tripped enough of them to make the witness let down his or her guard. I was frequently amazed by what slipped out of witnesses mouths when they forgot they were in a courtroom."

Pat responded. "Think that'll work with Donald Maplewood?"

"I don't know. He's smart, but his brain doesn't make fine distinctions. The way to get him to lower his guard is to reach him at his simplistic level. At least, that's what I'm hoping."

They turned north at Bennington onto 7A and in twenty minutes came to Donald Maplewood's farm, basking organically in the sun. The low ridges bordering the farm to the west and the final thrusts of the Taconics on the east cradled the fields. Jim slowed the car. Donald did not know they were coming.

They could see a man working the field nearest the farmhouse, but on closer inspection, it wasn't Donald. Then they saw Donald leave the house through what Jim remembered as the kitchen door.

Jim pulled into the driveway, making Donald stop and look to see who was coming. Jim parked the car, and he and Pat got out. Striding forward, Jim waved as if they were on a friendly visit.

Donald approached. He did not look friendly.

"What do you want?"

"To talk to you."

"I thought I made myself clear. I have nothing more to say to you."

Jim gestured to Pat, standing beside him. "I think you two have met. Pat Knowles, my former colleague."

Donald nodded. "We have."

"Can we talk inside? I could use some water."

Donald scoffed. "No. We talk here." They were standing in the driveway. The lone man was still working the nearest field.

"What's he doing? I can't tell."

In spite of himself, Donald turned to look. "Jake? Pulling weeds. Nice try but it won't work. Speak your piece and do it quickly, or I'm gone. I have a farm to run."

"Does your father's company own your farm?"

"Yes. That's no secret. Dad helped me buy the farm when I was floundering in my life."

"And will Stan Mitchell's private equity firm own your farm once it acquires Maplewood Farms?"

"Yes, but I'll still run it. That's part of the deal."

"For how long? I can't imagine private equity stakeholders being content with meager profits. Won't they sell it?"

"I'm small fry. They won't care enough about my farm to sell it. I'm not worried." He gave a sputter of a laugh, a one-cylinder laugh.

"Do you mind if we talk in the fields?"

Donald looked startled. "A judge? Wants to talk in a field? Why on earth? No pun intended."

"We don't have fields in Cambridge. They're a nice change of pace. Okay?" True, but not the real reason; the real reason was that Donald's guard would be lowered in the fields.

Donald peered closely at Jim, then shrugged. "Okay."

Pat said she would wait in the car. "I'm not wearing the right shoes."

Jim nodded. "We won't be long."

"Take your time."

Jim followed Donald onto the field. The earth felt spongy beneath his feet.

"Bibb lettuce. High quality. Fetches a premium in stores. This is far enough. Speak your peace," Donald said when they reached the middle of the field.

"Standing between earth and sun, I can almost feel the world turning, know what I mean?"

"I suppose," Donald said.

"Course not. You're used to it. Let me ask, when you took up farming, did your father understand?"

Donald started to speak, then stopped. "I don't know."

"He didn't express an opinion?"

Donald walked a step or two. He had to step carefully between the rows of young lettuce. "He thought I should join him in the business side of the company. Said I could run it when he retired."

"That didn't appeal to you?"

"Nope. Partly because I feared I wouldn't be as good a manager as Dad, and partly because I liked farming."

Jim nodded sympathetically. "Standing here I can see why. Sun and soil. Educate me how organic farming differs from conventional farming. Does it simply mean food grown without pesticides?"

"That's the bare-bones definition. A lot more goes into it. The pests that destroy crops aren't grateful, they don't back off if you don't use pesticides. So it's a never-ending battle between remaining 'pure' for the market and your crop being eaten by pests. It's much more labor intensive and the yields don't match the non-organic kind."

"You use no pesticides? Ever?"

"No pesticides. We poison rats. I'm not willing to turn the other cheek to rats. They are nasty, vicious animals. But no pesticides. Seen enough?"

"Not quite. Before we go back to your house, I'd like to see the barn where you keep your equipment."

"You want to see the barn where I keep my equipment? Why? There's nothing special about it."

"I like to understand how things work. Humor me."

Jim followed Donald to the first of several outbuildings big and small scattered about the property. They passed several small structures – "tool sheds," Donald explained. He seemed to be enjoying himself again. Beyond a tree break, they came to a broad field that would yield corn into the early fall. On the other side of the field stood a good-sized barn.

Donald and Jim approached the barn, Jim by now feeling as to the farm-life-born. The house and road could not be seen from the barn. "In here, I keep my tractors. My pride and joy." Donald slid open the door. Jim smelled hay as soon as they walked in, but what he saw were tractors, big and small, and various implements, including spindly planters and bulky roller harrows. Donald beamed with pride and patted a giant John Deere on its flanks. "This baby is my favorite."

"Very impressive," Jim said. "Mind if I look around?"

"Help yourself. If you have any questions, let me know."

Jim circled the barn, peering closely at the implements. He didn't know what he was looking for but was convinced he'd find it in the barn. A ladder led up to a small ledge, and the rear wall of the barn was lined with closet-like storage bins. He went to one of them and asked, "What's in here?" Without waiting for an answer, he opened the nearest door and saw a storage closet with shelves. Bottles and cans of various sizes overflowed the shelves. Several of the cans displayed a skull and crossbones.

"Is this what you use on rats?" Jim pointed to the one of cans.

"Yep," Donald said. "Brutal but effective. Kills over the course of a few days. The rats go nuts trying to get to water and eventually die from internal bleeding. Let me show you something over here."

He led Jim to a corner where a tall piece of equipment leaned against the wall. "Invented this myself," Donald explained what it was, but Jim wasn't listening. Finally, Donald noticed. "Had enough?"

"Yes. You've been generous with your time."

They left the barn. "I still don't get what you were after. Why drive all the way here? What were you hoping to find?"

"I don't always know what I'm looking for. My method is to collect as many pieces of the puzzle as I can and assemble them only when I've got them all."

"And do you now?"

"I think so."

Donald seemed relaxed as they walked back across the fields. Time for the nail-in-the-coffin question. Jim waited to ask until he and Donald were standing next to Jim's car in the driveway.

"What did Glen Hudson think of the farm when he came to check it out?"

Donald smirked. "You should've seen the look on his face when he got mud on his city shoes. But I think he was impressed with how well I run the farm."

"I can see why. I'm sure he told Stan Mitchell it was worth acquiring. Thanks, Donald. You've been helpful."

Jim climbed in his car. Neither Pat nor Jim spoke until they turned east at Bennington.

Pat spoke first. "How did you know Glen Hudson had been to the farm?"

"I didn't. What I knew was that a diabetic is at risk of dying if his blood sugar levels get far enough out of balance, and that certain kinds of poisons in very low doses can trigger such an imbalance. The beauty of it is that no one suspects poisoning."

More silence. Silence until they approached Brattleboro.

Again Pat. "So, do you know whodunnit?"

"I have a strong suspicion."

Pat stared at him. "Are you going to tell me, or are you going sit there looking smug?"

"You don't like my smug look? Okay, here goes. To acquire Maplewood Naturals, Stan Mitchell had to get Arthur Maplewood out of the way. As a man experienced in acquiring companies, willing and unwilling, I'm sure Mitchell learned all he could about his targets, and one thing I'm sure he learned was that Maplewood was a diabetic. Mitchell had Glen Hudson take it from there, and Hudson discovered that rat poison in small doses was one of the poisons that could kill a diabetic while making the death appear to be from natural causes. Whether Hudson learned that before or after his visit to Donald Maplewood's farm, I don't know, but my guess is that when Glen Hudson saw the rat poison in Donald's barn, it sealed the deal. Hudson had plenty of opportunity after that to poison Arthur Maplewood. He met with Arthur several times trying to persuade him to sell Maplewood Naturals to Mitchell Equity. It would have been easy to slip Arthur small doses of poison at each meeting to interfere with his blood sugar level. Ergo, Arthur Maplewood was out of the way and no one was the wiser."

"An autopsy would answer a lot of questions," Pat said.

"Precisely my thinking."

"But how to obtain one when either Vanessa or Donald can block it?"

"Ted could seek a court order, but I'll talk to Vanessa and tell her what I've discovered, see if she changes her mind. Want to visit the Big Apple again?"

*

The contrast of the scalloped beauty of the Connecticut shoreline and the ugliness of Penn Station struck him as forcefully as ever. Why does New York City tolerate it? Jim and Pat wheeled their carry-ons past the most depressing food joints in the world and waited in line for a taxi.

"What time did Vanessa agree to see us?"

"5."

Pat looked at her watch. "Plenty of time."

They stayed at the same hotel as before. Pat liked to get to places far in advance so they left the hotel at 4:30 for the short walk to Vanessa's offices. Delivery vans clogged the street in front of her building.

Vanessa greeted them with wary cordiality. "Nice to see you again. Please sit down."

The three of them sat on translucent chairs.

"Did Donald tell you we visited his farm again?" Jim began.

"No. We haven't talked recently."

"I'm closing in on proof that your father was poisoned, most likely by Glen Hudson acting on behalf of Stan Mitchell. I believe an autopsy can answer the remaining questions. You vetoed an autopsy before, will you change your mind now that I'm near a solution?"

Vanessa studied her hands. Her expression didn't change. "No."

"Why? If your father was murdered, surely you want to know."

"Why are you asking me now, after you visited Donald's farm? You found something, didn't you?"

"Yes."

"You found the poison you think was used, didn't you?"

"Yes. Rat poison in small doses can kill by interfering with a diabetic's control of his blood sugar, without looking like poisoning. That fits the scenario in your father's death."

"You found the poison that killed my father at my brother's farm, and you are asking me to okay an autopsy that may implicate my brother?"

"Finding it on Donald's farm doesn't mean Donald supplied it to Glen Hudson. It can be found in any farm supply store."

"But you think otherwise."

"My guess is that Hudson had been looking for a hard-to-detect way to kill your father and seeing the rat poison on your brother's farm triggered Hudson's thinking. Whether your brother knew what Glen Hudson had in mind is another matter."

Vanessa shook her head. "I think you missed your calling, Judge Randall. Audacity is equally as important as talent in the fashion business, and you've got plenty of audacity."

"But no fashion sense," Pat couldn't help saying.

"I can see that." Vanessa scoffed. "I'll make a deal with you, Judge Randall. If you can get Donald to agree to an autopsy, I'll take that as a sign that he played no role in Dad's death, and I'll give you my okay."

Jim called Donald from the hotel. He waited until after dinner. "Hell, no," and a dead phone were Donald's answer.

"Hard to tell whether he's pissed at my meddling or hiding something," Jim told Pat after the call.

"Maybe both."

"I'll sit down with Ted when we get back. I don't have much hope he'll say yes to obtaining a court order, but I have to try."

Ted was in the middle of a high-profile trial that was expected to last a week. "Can it wait until next week?" he texted when Jim asked to see him.

They arranged to meet first thing Monday. Over the weekend, Jim became fatalistic about the outcome. "He'll say no. I would."

"Jim, I say this to you as your lover, confidant, and biggest supporter. You need a break. You've cut corners in this investigation you normally wouldn't, because you're too caught up in it. Let's take a vacation."

"Can't."

"Why not?"

"My obsessiveness won't allow it."

"I insist."

They compromised on a long weekend.

"Not to Vermont," she added. "Someplace new for us."

They went to the Cape. Not easy to find a room on the spur of the moment, but they lucked out and called a motel just as someone else cancelled. Jim had been to the Cape a handful of times and didn't love it. He hated to lie on a beach in the hot sun. The ocean was soothing he admitted, but sand and sun were aggravating.

The motel they booked had a pool and deck chairs with mammoth umbrellas. Jim settled into a deck chair as soon as they arrived and basically didn't move for three days. Pat would look at him once in a while to be sure he was alive, and be reassured by the rise and fall of the open book on his stomach. A straw hat rested at an angle on his head, half-covering his eyes. He had enough hair left to protect his head and normally didn't wear hats, but on the Cape, sitting in a deck chair, a hat seemed appropriate. From time to time, she would nudge his foot to get him to stop snoring.

"You've been asleep a long time," she said when he opened his eyes.

"I wasn't asleep. My eyes were closed, but I wasn't asleep."

"Then why were you snoring?"

"To fool you. Worked, didn't it?"

She waited a beat to let him regroup. "I'm glad we came, aren't you?"

"Okay, okay, I was asleep. Satisfied?"

"When you're ready, Jim, we'll go to dinner."

He sat upright in the deck chair. "It's that late?"

They ate at a quiet place that mimicked a New England inn. Nice try, but it didn't work. White tablecloths in a land of sand don't convey what white tablecloths are meant to convey.

But they had a fine time. Stalled on the case, Jim moved forward on the home front, i.e., became sentimental.

"We work as a couple, don't we? We get along pretty well. We don't fight."

"Not usually," Pat agreed.

"We share each other's values. We have mutual respect. These things are important, aren't they." Jim asked the questions without spoken question marks.

"They certainly are. And you're not intimidated by me. That's important."

"Was your late husband?"

"No. But he had his own professional world. We loved each other but didn't move in the same worlds. It saved a lot of conflict."

"Joyce and I tolerated each other. We spent our first married years trying to find a mutual rhythm but eventually gave up. There were values we didn't share. But we loved each other in our own way."

They skipped desert in favor of an early bedtime. They had to get up before dawn to drive back to Cambridge for Jim's meeting with Ted.

15

Not for the first time, Jim noted that you couldn't tell much about Ted Conover by his office. A few (but not many) pictures of his family on his desk, an oil painting of a sailboat on the wall behind his desk. You could leave the office after a long meeting and have a hard time describing where you had been. Jim thought that was one of the ways Ted had survived so long in the bureaucracy. Low profile coupled with high performance equals longevity.

Ted liked to sit at his desk when holding a meeting, even when meeting with a friend and former colleague. He frowned when Jim described finding rat poison in Donald Maplewood's barn and learning that Glen Hudson had visited the farm before Arthur Maplewood's death.

"I see where you're going with this. You seek an exhumation and autopsy of Maplewood."

"That's right."

"Even if I were inclined to grant your request, either of the next-of-kin can veto it."

"Yes. In that case, it takes a court order."

Ted stood and began pacing. Ted rarely paced without a reason, and Jim thought the reason this time was that Ted was torn between his desire to help an old friend and his professional obligations as an assistant DA.

Jim tried to help him out. "There is a strong circumstantial case that Glen Hudson poisoned Arthur Maplewood at the instigation of Stan Mitchell. Mitchell's nurse overheard an incriminating conversation shortly before Glen Hudson visited Donald Maplewood's farm, and while at the farm, Hudson saw rat poison in Donald's barn."

Ted stopped pacing. "It's still too circumstantial. I need to nail it down before I'm willing to seek a court order."

"I'll do my best to nail it."

"Angry at me?"

"No, we're good friends, so I'll cut you some slack."

Ted laughed. "Big of you, considering you are the one who lacks the crucial evidence."

"You know me. All heart."

Jim walked to The Long Gone after he left Ted's office, surprised not to find a groove in the sidewalk from the many times he had walked the same route.

The Long Gone was full. Nowhere to sit. Standing, Jim had a moment to reflect – this place that seemed so familiar now had been unknown to him before he retired from the court. Hard to believe.

He ordered a coffee to go and took it outside searching for a place to sit. There was a bench in front of the coffeehouse, but it was occupied by a young man absorbed in the conversation he was having with himself or someone on the other end of an unseen cellphone. There were benches in a triangular park at the intersection, but a scraggly man was sleeping on one of the benches and the traffic made the park noisy. The first quiet space with an unoccupied bench was beside the hospital a block and a half away.

He sat on the bench with his coffee and a sigh, removed the lid from the coffee and took a sip. Lukewarm coffee and a depleted brain do not a happy ex-judge make.

What if Ted turned him down? What then? He calculated the odds and decided they were not good. Give up?

Why not? Admit defeat. Take up needlepoint.

He felt a buzzing in his pocket. He pulled out his phone. I must have put it on vibrate, he rebuked himself.

"Hello?"

"Jim, it's Ted. Okay."

"Okay, what?"

"I've thought about it, and I'll okay an autopsy."

"That was quick."

"I saw no point in delay. I don't anticipate this will be easy. I'm assuming one or more of his next-of-kin will object and I'll have to go to a judge."

"I'm very relieved. Thank you. I hope like hell this does not come back to haunt you."

"Me too. Wish us both luck."

Jim remained seated on the bench after Ted's call. He stared straight ahead without seeing anything. Joyce had died in this hospital. Good omen? Bad omen?

He stood, testing his legs, and walked the rest of the way home.

Pat spent the night at his house, and they ate dinner watching *PBS Newshour* with the sound on mute. "How long do you anticipate it will take Ted?"

"Depends on his workload and the obstacles he encounters. A week? Maybe longer."

*

Jim busied himself as best he could while waiting, but his constitution did not easily permit diversion. Good at buckling down, not good at easing off. He tried to catch up on the books piled on his bedside table, but he couldn't concentrate on anything difficult. When in doubt, read a Maigret. Chief Inspector Maigret of the Paris Judiciaire solved crimes by getting inside the minds of suspects, and did it in Paris with his favorite café nearby and his endlessly patient wife waiting for him at home with coq au vin simmering on the stove. Jim had The Long Gone, Pat across the river, and Duck, Duck, Goose around the corner. Not the same, but not bad for an ex-judge in Cambridge, Massachusetts.

"I hate waiting." Jim slammed his book shut a week after Ted's phone call.

"Calm down, Jim. Ted's doing everything he can."

Chagrined, Jim shifted gears. "Where's my coq au vin?"

"Excuse me?" Pat's voice sounded amused.

"Want to move to Paris? They have lots of sidewalk cafes. I wouldn't miss The Long Gone."

"Jim, what has gotten into you?"

Jim reached for the phone. "I can't wait any longer. I'm calling Ted."

Ted answered as if he had been expecting Jim's call. "No go, so far. Donald Maplewood adamantly refused an autopsy and Vanessa won't go along unless her brother does. I've got staffers working on a court order now. I have to tell you, Jim, this is going to be close."

"I'm grateful to you for trying."

"You'd better be. When I retire I hope I'm not a thorn in the side of a tired public servant who just wants to do his job and go home."

"You're saying I'm a thorn?"

"If the metaphor fits. I'll get back to you as soon as I have news."

Pat waited for a report after Jim got off the phone. When Jim remained silent, she said, "No go?"

"Not so far. Donald said no, which triggered a no from Vanessa. Ted's office is working on a court order. He is not brimming with confidence, it's fair to say."

*

By the end of another week, Jim was going nuts. Serenity, equanimity – where art thou? He had neither when young, so why should he expect them now? Dammit, the old were entitled to them! That's why. He banged his gavel to close the case.

Ted's call came on Friday.

"A court hearing on my motion has been scheduled for next Thursday. Can you be there?"

"Let me check my calendar."

"What?"

"I'm kidding. Of course I'll be there. What time?"

"Nine a.m. Sorry to have kept you waiting on this, Jim. But I have to admit I got a kick out of picturing you pacing the floor and cursing my name."

"I didn't pace and curse. I sat and fumed."

*

Jim had presided over plenty of hearings as a judge. Usually the courtroom was empty except for the attorneys who were arguing the case. Several things about this hearing were unusual. One was the presence in the courtroom of two retired judges, Jim and Pat. Another was the tension in the room, tension visible in the faces of Glen Hudson, Donald Maplewood, Vanessa Maplewood, and their lawyer, a seasoned litigator named Harold Rawlings. Rawlings was known to dissect an opposing lawyer's arguments with a scalpel so sharp that no blood flowed until after the hearing.

The presiding judge was Jessica Haynes, new to the court since Jim and Pat retired. In Jim's eyes, Judge Haynes looked eighteen. She lifted her head to signal a start to the proceedings. "Mr. Conover?"

"Good morning, your honor." Ted Conover rose to his feet and buttoned his jacket. "The people are requesting a court order to exhume the remains of Arthur Maplewood in order to more precisely determine the cause of death."

"Point of order, your honor." Harold Rawlings was on his feet.

Judge Haynes responded, "So soon, Mr. Rawlings?"

"Yes, your honor."

"Proceed."

"We protest the presence of two retired judges from this very court in the courtroom. It is unusual to say the least."

"The judges in question retired before I was appointed to this bench. I have never met them."

"Yes, your honor, but they served on this court."

"I understand your point, but I deny your request. You may proceed, Mr. Conover."

"Thank you, your honor," Ted said. "Briefly stated, the facts of this case are this: Within days of each other, two archrivals died: Arthur Maplewood and his nemesis,

Stan Mitchell. Stan Mitchell died on stage at his law school reunion, at which he was the honoree. According to the medical examiner, Mitchell died of a pacemaker malfunction causing his weak heart to fail. Arthur Maplewood died several days later from complications of diabetes, again according to the medical examiner. The two men had a long history of personal and business animosity – Mitchell's private equity firm was trying to acquire Maplewood's company, and Maplewood had filed an ethics complaint against Mitchell for his tactics in the attempted takeover. Maplewood's death removed the major obstacle to the takeover, and Mitchell's death made moot the ethics complaint."

Ted had been standing in front of the judge, a page of notes in his hands. He turned now and gestured to Donald and Vanessa.

"Your honor, since Stan Mitchell died before Arthur Maplewood, he cannot be questioned on his role, if any, in Arthur Maplewood's death. Which is one of the reasons it is so important to determine by autopsy the exact cause of Arthur Maplewood's death. If his death was, indeed, the result of natural causes, we can close the books on this case. If, on the other hand, there is evidence of foul play, the Commonwealth has an obligation to try his killer or killers and, at least provisionally, block the acquisition of Maplewood Naturals by Mitchell Equity. Without an autopsy we'll never know, which may result in a grave miscarriage of justice. Thank you, Your Honor."

Ted returned to his table but didn't get a chance to sit down since Attorney Rawlings waived his opening statement until after the Commonwealth's witnesses were heard.

"In that case, you may proceed with your witnesses, Mr. Conover," Judge Haynes said.

"Only one, Your Honor. Retired judge Jim Randall."

Jim rose and strode forward. As he did, he marveled at the fact that during his long career he had been a judge, a defense attorney, and now a witness – a utility infielder of the legal profession.

He mounted the witness stand. How different a courtroom looked from this height and angle.

Ted: "State your name for the record, please."

"James Randall."

"Until your retirement, you served as a judge on the Massachusetts Superior Court?"

"Yes, for twenty-one years."

Ted turned and took two steps back. "Please tell the court how and why you became involved in this case."

Jim's throat was dry. He wished he had taken a sip of water before he took the witness stand. "Since my retirement, I have investigated cases that interested me and where I thought I could be of help because of my experience as a judge. What got me involved in this particular case was being at the reunion where Stan Mitchell died as he was being honored by his class. I had known Stan in law school and seeing him die on stage was a profound shock. When I read that Arthur Maplewood died a few days later, I was intrigued. That is the kind of coincidence that catches my attention. So I started looking into the deaths."

"And what did you find?"

"I spoke to the Mitchell siblings, Donald and Vanessa, and to Glen Hudson, Stan Mitchell's business partner. The timeline of Glen Hudson's actions indicate that he had the opportunity, the means, and the incentive to murder Arthur Maplewood. I believe the means of murder was small doses of rat poison administered to Arthur Maplewood when Hudson met with him over a period of time on behalf of Stan Mitchell. Arthur Maplewood was a diabetic and the poison interfered with his blood sugar control, leading to his death. Hudson may have obtained the poison on Donald Maplewood's farm, although it is possible that Hudson got the idea of using poison from his visits there but obtained the poison elsewhere, given its widespread availability. Those are questions that could be answered by a criminal prosecution."

Ted asked, "You said Glen Hudson had incentive to murder. What in your opinion was the incentive?"

"I believe his longtime partner and mentor Stan Mitchell wanted Arthur Maplewood dead to remove the major roadblock to a takeover, and to exact revenge for Maplewood's ethics complaint against him. And I believe that Mitchell enlisted his loyal lieutenant, Glen Hudson, to carry out his wish. Hudson had a personal motive, in addition to his loyalty: he was slated to become the controlling partner in Mitchell's private equity firm when Mitchell retired or died."

Ted returned to his table and turned to face Jim. "Judge Randall, you will undoubtedly be asked this question by Mr. Hudson's attorney, so I'll ask it first. Stan Mitchell died before Arthur Maplewood, therefore didn't stand to personally gain from Maplewood's death. How does that square with your explanation?"

"That was the question which troubled me the most. Here's what I believe. Stan Mitchell was a very sick man. He had round the clock nursing care for months before his death. Knowing he would die soon of natural causes, Stan Mitchell set Arthur Maplewood's murder in motion before hastening his own death, and by so doing, got rid of a hated rival and removed himself from suspicion for the murder. Who would suspect a dead man?"

Ted waited a moment to let Jim's testimony sink in, then stepped forward. "Your honor, an autopsy will determine whether Arthur Maplewood was poisoned, and if so, what kind of poison was used. We recognize the emotional pain an exhumation of a loved one's remains can cause family members, but we believe that the Commonwealth's interests in seeing that justice is served outweigh the family's temporary emotional distress in this case."

"Thank you, Mr. Conover. Mr. Rawlings?"

Rawlings rose from his seat at the defendant's table. "Thank you, your honor. Hello, Judge Randall, how are you?"

"Just fine, thank you."

Rawlings approached the witness stand. "Your powers of imagination are impressive, but in order for what you say to be true, split-second timing would be required so that the deaths were sequenced properly. God forbid that Arthur Maplewood should predecease Stan Mitchell. The finger of suspicion would then point to Mitchell. So how did Stan Mitchell time his death and Arthur Maplewood's so accurately?"

Jim replied, "He took his chances on when exactly Maplewood would die, but he had complete control of the timing of his own death. According to the medical examiner, Stan Mitchell's death was the result of a faulty pacemaker. I interviewed the nurse who took care of him in his final days, and she revealed that Mitchell's pacemaker was worn externally, unlike most pacemakers which are implanted in a patient's chest. All Mitchell had to do was pull the plugs on his pacemaker, knowing that his heart was so weak and defective that it would stop beating in a matter of hours, if not minutes. Stan being Stan, he killed himself in front of a celebratory audience. Arthur Maplewood's poisoning was already in motion by then, so Stan Mitchell could die knowing he had gotten away with murder."

"Very entertaining, Judge Randall. I see a TV miniseries. But do you have a shred of proof?"

"The Commonwealth is asking for an autopsy, not a conviction."

"So you have no proof?"

"I have witnesses who will confirm in court what I've said if an autopsy proves that Maplewood had poison in his system."

"I think that's a no." Rawlings turned to the judge and spread his arms wide. "They have no proof, your honor. Let's label this request for what it is, a fishing expedition."

"Call it what you will, Mr. Rawlings, but I'm inclined to side with the Commonwealth. The Commonwealth has an interest in seeing that justice is done. I advise you to heed Judge Randall's reminder: an autopsy is being sought, not a conviction."

"Are you making a ruling, your honor?"

"No, I'm not ready to, but I'm inclined to grant the Commonwealth's request. No lasting harm will be done to any living person. Anything else at the moment? If not, we'll adjourn until tomorrow at nine a.m. I'll announce my decision then."

*

Judge Haynes granted the Commonwealth's request the next morning, and Arthur Maplewood's remains were exhumed a week later. The autopsy that followed revealed rat poison in Arthur Maplewood's body, not enough to kill a healthy man but enough to trigger cardiac arrest in a diabetic.

Based on the autopsy, Ted obtained a subpoena to search Glen Hudson's penthouse in downtown Boston.

Ted called Jim after the search. "You were right. Traces of rat poison were found in Hudson's closet and on a windbreaker. He wasn't very careful about disposing of evidence. Shows his lack of criminal experience."

"Thank you for all you've done, Ted. Not only do you not stop me from meddling, you occasionally abandon good sense and do what I ask."

"You're lucky that it sometimes pans out. Otherwise I'd be forced to lock you up for meddling in the first degree."

"What now?"

"We go to trial. Don't worry, you'll be the star witness. Don't want to deprive you of your moment of glory."

"Sarcasm will get you nowhere, my friend. You need to learn dignity."

"Like you used to have before you turned sleuth?"

"Yes, like that."

16

Donald Maplewood pled guilty to being an accessory to murder for providing Glen Hudson with the rat poison, and was sentenced to two years in prison and six years of probation. The sentencing judge took into account Donald's emotional plea that he didn't know for sure why Glen Hudson wanted the rat poison, that he assumed the reason had to do with a rat problem Hudson claimed to be having at his country house.

In exchange for his cooperation with the prosecution, Glen Hudson was charged with second-degree murder instead of first-degree. When Hudson testified, he blamed everything on Stan Mitchell, claiming that Mitchell came up with the scheme to kill Arthur Maplewood by throwing his blood sugar out of control. In spite of the fact that Hudson stood to head Maplewood Naturals if Mitchell's scheme succeeded, Hudson denied having any personal interest in Maplewood's demise. He said he agreed to the scheme only to placate the dying Stan Mitchell. A key witness in the trial was Maria Hernandez, who testified she overheard Hudson tell Mitchell that, in his opinion, the stockholders of Maplewood Naturals would vote to sell the company to Mitchell Equity if Arthur Maplewood were out of the way. She made a very credible witness. Jim gave her a lot of credit: he had placed some phone calls before she testified and could reassure Maria that her visa extension wouldn't be jeopardized if she testified; still, it took guts and a certain amount of trust. Jim testified at length, recounting in detail how and why he became involved and what he had learned, starting with the shock of seeing Stan Mitchell die on stage as he was being honored by his law school class, and ending with his visit to Donald Maplewood's farm. After Jim stepped down from the witness stand, he decided he liked being a judge better than being a witness.

The jury deliberated for less than a day before rendering its verdict of guilty. Glen Hudson's sentencing hearing was scheduled in two weeks. Jim and Pat repaired to the Vermont house to await the hearing.

The intense green of summer had faded from relentless sun and too little rain, and the bright colors of fall were still in hiding. It was if a pause button had been hit between seasons. The light over the Connecticut River valley seemed conflicted, unsure, waiting for direction. When the light wicked out each evening, it seemed to do so out of exhaustion, of ennui.

Jim and Pat watched the light, ate their dinners, rarely spoke. When they did, they spoke in halting non-sequiturs, their ideas supply having run dry:

"This investigation took a lot out of me."

"It is sad to see what greed can do to a family."

"If I ever play sleuth again, I'll pick a case where there is one death, and only one death."

"I like this wine. What is it?"

*

Glen Hudson received a sentence of life imprisonment, with the possibility of parole after twenty-five years. The look on his face when he heard the sentence was one of shock, anger, and disbelief. Stan Mitchell would undoubtedly have been convicted of first degree murder, which carries a sentence of life without possibility of parole, but dead men can't be convicted.

30620271R00104